"You slept with my sister, Mr. Kendall."

He leaned forward, and the black threat on his face made Leigh draw back sharply.

"Yes, I did, Miss Walker. Two consenting adults. And if you're going to try and blackmail me, then you're barking up the wrong tree."

"I have no intention of blackmailing you, Mr. Kendall." Just what sort of world did this man move in, where blackmail featured on the menu? "I've come here to break some rather...unexpected news. I've come to tell you that you're a father. You have a seven-year-old daughter. Her name is Amy."

Dear Reader,

A perfect nanny can be tough to find, but once you've found her you'll love and treasure her forever. She's someone who'll not only look after the kids but also could be that loving mom they never knew. Or sometimes she's a he and is the daddy they are wishing for.

Here at Harlequin Presents® we've put together a compelling series, NANNY WANTED!, in which some of our most popular authors create nannies whose talents extend way beyond taking care of the children! Each story will excite and delight you and make you wonder how any family could be complete without a nineties nanny.

Remember—nanny knows best when it comes to falling in love!

The Editors

Look out next month for:

A Nanny for Christmas by Sara Craven (#1999)

CATHY WILLIAMS

A Daughter for Christmas

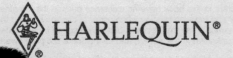

ISBN 0-373-11993-3

A DAUGHTER FOR CHRISTMAS

First North American Publication 1998.

CHAPTER ONE

THE decision to contact Nicholas Kendall had been a difficult one, arrived at after months of soul-searching and after every other option had been exhausted.

Or at least as far as Leigh could see.

And then there had been the big question of how precisely to establish contact. Should she telephone him? It was too big an issue to deal with over the phone. Should she just find out where he lived and pay him a surprise visit? No, he might die from shock. She had no idea how old he was or, for that matter, what the state of his heart was. So she was left with the ubiquitous letter.

But, then, how much should she say? Enough to arouse his curiosity but not so much that he dismissed the situation without a second glance. After all, she knew precious little about the man.

Jenny had told her about him in one shocking emotional outburst, but a hospital bed had been no place to ask all those questions that had forced themselves to the surface, shattering in ten charged minutes the calm, contented surface which had comprised her sister's life. And now there was no Jenny around to tell her anything at all.

She had posted the letter ten days ago. Now, holding his reply in her hand, she felt exactly as she'd imagined she would. Unsure. Had she done the right thing? Had she betrayed her sister's confidence or would she have understood? She stared down at the sheet of thick paper, at the black handwriting and wished she hadn't found herself forced into this corner.

'What's the matter?'

Leigh looked up from the letter and hurriedly stuffed it into the pocket of her cardigan, then she shook her head and smiled down at the child, staring earnestly up at her.

'Nothing. Have you brushed your hair, Ames? You can't go to school looking like that.' She looked fondly at her niece and tried to eliminate the traces of worry from her face. Children could be unnervingly clever at picking up shades of feeling, and the more Amy was spared the better. She had already been through enough.

'It's the house, isn't it?' Amy said in a small voice. 'They're going to take the house away from us, aren't they?'

'What on earth makes you say that?' Leigh felt her heart sink.

'I heard you talking to Carol about it on the phone last night.'

They stared at each other and, not for the first time, Leigh felt an overwhelming sensation of helplessness. Helplessness in the face of events over which she had no control. Helplessness at being caught up in a cyclone. Helplessness at being unable to run away because there was Amy, her sister's daughter, who needed looking after. Oh, God, how on earth was she ever going to explain what was going on?

'You should have been asleep, Amy!'

Amy didn't say anything. She just stood there in her winter school uniform. Seven years old, with long dark hair and solemn, green eyes.

'Yes, darling, there *are* a few problems with the house. I'm working on it.'

'Will we have to move out?'

'We'll see.' She paused and sighed. 'We might, yes.'

'But you won't leave me, will you?' she asked in a high whisper, and Leigh knelt on the ground and took the child's face between her hands. It wasn't the first time that she had had to do this—to persuade her niece that she wasn't about to disappear, that she'd be there when evening came and when the following morning rolled around as well. The school psychologist had told Leigh that it was a reaction she could expect and one which could last for years after the deaths of Amy's parents—a need to be reassured and a tendency to cling like ivy to the support systems that remained in her life.

'No chance, dwarf,' Leigh said soberly. 'You're stuck with me, like it or not. Now, your hair. Then breakfast, then school. At this rate we'll never get this show off the road.' She smoothed back the long hair from Amy's face and kissed her forehead. 'And *hurry*. You know what Mrs Stephens is like when it comes to punctuality! I shall have another lecture on time-keeping and then *I* shall be late for work.'

She went downstairs and prepared breakfast, acting as normally as she could, and all the while that little letter burnt a hole in her pocket.

Nicholas Kendall had agreed to meet her. In two days' time. At his club in the City. There had been no questions asked, and she assumed that he was waiting—waiting to see what turned up. He must be curious, but there had been no hint of it in his note. No hint of anything at all, in fact. Nothing to tell her what sort of man he was.

She wished she had had the foresight to ask Jenny a few more questions at the time, but the circumstances following the accident had been so overwhelming and the confession so startling that all she had done was listen in amazement.

'I'm sorry, Leigh,' her sister had said weakly, her breathing shallow. 'I know that this is a shock but I don't want to leave, carrying this secret with me. I *can't* do that to you. I need to tell you, need to explain…'

And Leigh hadn't asked a thing. She had been too aghast at what she had been hearing. *Roy* had been Amy's father. Amy's father and Jenny's husband. Or so she had always thought.

Now she was being told that it had all been an illusion. A third party had been brought in, some man she had never heard of in her life before. It had been a one-night stand, Jenny had said, a moment's impulse when she had been driven by despair and desperation, a moment's insanity that she and Roy had put behind them, but all things came home to roost in the end, didn't they?

Leigh desperately wished that she had asked questions, instead of simply sitting there, mouth agape, as though this sort of thing didn't happen all the time. All she had been told by her sister during her last, frantic jumbled ramblings had been the man's name and the fact that he lived in London.

And Leigh had stuffed the insidious information to the back of her mind for well over a year and a half.

At first it had been easy just to bury the name she had scribbled on that piece of paper to the back of a drawer. There had been so much to do, arrangements to be made, and, of course, Amy to look after now both her parents were dead. One minute Leigh had been cruising along, going to art school, planning a future as a graphic artist in some advertising firm—dreaming her dreams—and the next minute she'd been handed the mantle of responsibility.

Almost immediately the financial problems had reared up, like a freakish, multi-headed monster, twisting in every direction and blocking all the exits. The painting and decorating business, which had been Roy's domain, and the interior design side of it, which had been Jenny's—both of which Leigh had naïvely thought had been doing well—had been breaking under the weight of the economic recession.

Their accountant had given Leigh precisely one week's reprieve after the funeral, before calling her and laying all the cards on the table.

Leigh had sat through it all in a daze. She'd had no idea of finance and had stared in bewilderment at the sheets of figures which had been produced for her to see.

'Can't we just find someone else to run it?' she had asked a little wildly. 'I mean, what's going to happen to the men in the company? Bob and Nicky and Dan?'

'What happens to all people who find themselves out of work.' The accountant had shrugged, not entirely unsympathetic but businesslike. 'There's no point, employing someone to try and rescue the business,' he had told her in a kinder voice.

'Think about it. It doesn't make sense, does it? To spend money hiring someone for a business that's in the process of failing. There have been no new orders for your sister's side of things since...' he glanced down at a sheet of paper '...the middle of the year. No one wants to spend money on redesigning the insides of their houses!'

'But it can't fail! There's Amy! *I* can't help with money! I'm still at college...'

'You could always put your studies on hold for a while, try and see what you can do. I'll give you my services free...'

That had been one and a half years ago and she had given it everything she had. She had abandoned her beloved dreams of a career in art and had taken an interminably mundane office job, the only merit of which was that it brought some money in. And it seemed as though, overnight, she had aged into an old woman.

It hadn't been enough. The creditors, circling at first, had gradually moved in closer and closer. The bank had lost sympathy. By the time Ed, the accountant, advised her to let go, she was utterly defeated.

Heaven knows, she might have been able to carry on with the office job, scraping pennies together and dreaming her pointless dreams in the privacy of her head, but then the bank had foreclosed on their house, and that had been the last straw.

It was only then that the piece of paper, lying at the back of the drawer like some forgotten incantation, had begun to beckon.

She would be opening a can of worms and might well end up making things even worse than they already were, but the time had come for the gamble to be taken.

For the next two days Leigh wavered somewhere between dread and a despairing kind of forced optimism which would break down the minute she questioned it too closely.

In front of Amy she preserved a façade of carefree joviality, but it was a strain and once or twice she had caught her niece looking at her with huge, worried eyes. It hurt tremendously that there was very little she could do to reassure her, apart from promising faithfully never to leave her. That much she could do at least.

There were absolutely no other promises of security she could hope to offer, and she still hadn't decided what she would tell Amy when the time came for decisions

to be made. A lot rested on what this Nicholas Kendall had to say, whether some sort of meeting ground could be reached, but of that she held out very little hope.

What man, presented with the sudden appearance of a seven-year-old daughter he never knew existed, would greet the situation with a chuckle and open arms? The most she could hope for was someone who would at least hear her out.

But, Lord, she knew precious little about him, though considerably more than she had done a year and a half ago. She had done her homework, and it hadn't been that difficult to discover who he was—a mover and shaker in financial circles, a wealthy, dynamic man, apparently, whose listing in *Who's Who* had made her swallow with nerves. This, it seemed, was the man who had fathered her niece.

Oh, Jen, *why*? But there was no point in crying over spilt milk. Besides, she knew why.

She dressed very, very carefully that Friday morning. Admittedly, there wasn't much she could do with her face. It steadfastly resisted all attempts to be glamorised and she had faced that fact a long time ago. Her reddish-gold hair was too short to look chic, her eyes were too blue and too widely spaced to look feline and sexy and, of course, the freckles everywhere were the final straw. Winter or summer there they were, forever sabotaging her efforts to look her age—giving her the gamin-like appearance of an overgrown elf, or so she thought whenever she looked in the mirror.

She looked in the mirror now and concentrated on the wardrobe she had donned, wondering whether it looked right. She wasn't quite sure *what* she was aiming for, considering she had never met the man, but she knew

that whatever she wore would have to give her confidence.

Amy sat on the bed and watched Leigh while she fiddled with her long hair, brushing it and plaiting it.

'Where are you going?' she asked, when her hair had been neatly pulled away from her face and plaited.

'What makes you think that I'm going anywhere?'

'You don't normally take this long getting dressed.'

'Sometimes I do!' Leigh protested, glancing at the reflection of the child in the mirror and grinning. 'OK. I give in. Hardly ever. I just thought that this might make a nice change. What do you think?'

She twirled on the spot, holding one corner of the flowing red and black skirt between her fingers.

'You look beautiful,' Amy said honestly, and Leigh could have hugged her. 'Are you meeting someone?'

'Oh, you know, the usual.' She shrugged and smiled vaguely. 'What are you going to be doing in school today?' she asked, changing the subject.

'Maths, science, sports.' Their eyes met and Leigh smiled.

'Have you had the results of that test you had last week?'

'We get them today,' Amy said glumly.

'We can treat ourselves to a burger and a milkshake after school if you do OK,' Leigh said. A rare indulgence, she thought, and Amy deserved it. When times had been good she had had as many burgers and milkshakes as she could have eaten, and now that times were rocky she hadn't complained once about what she was now missing. She had just adapted, in that curious, malleable way children had, accepting their straitened circumstances without complaint.

'What if I do badly?' Amy asked with concern.

'Well, we'll treat ourselves anyway. Consolation prize, so to speak.' By four this afternoon, Leigh thought, I'll be in much the same boat myself. Whether things go well or not, I'll be just so damn relieved that a burger and milkshake will be just the thing.

'Anyway,' Leigh told her niece, as an afterthought, 'it doesn't matter whether you pass or fail that comprehension test, just so long as you put all your efforts into trying.'

'That's what Mrs Spencer keeps telling us.'

'Well, there you go, then. We can't both be wrong, can we?' She turned to the little figure on the bed and grinned reassuringly. What she saw, though, wasn't Amy sitting on the bed with folded legs, but Amy in the future, bombarded by revelations that would redefine the whole contours of her life.

She slipped the long-sleeved woollen turtleneck over her head and only inspected herself again when they were about to leave the house.

She looked, she decided, reasonably all right—neat and combed, at any rate, which for her made a change, and for once colour co-ordinated—black and red skirt, black, clingy turtleneck just showing under the black jumper, black coat because although it was only the end of October the weather was unseasonably cold and flat black shoes. Sober attire, she reflected. Highly appropriate, given the mission in hand.

Her first stop was to drop Amy off at school, then there was an hour and a half during which time she knew that she would simply freefall in a fever of apprehension. She had never been as strong and assertive as her sister. Jenny had always protected her from unsavoury problems, and it had only been in the last sixteen months or so that she had begun to show her own strengths.

Of course, it was the uncertainty which was gnawing away at her. She knew that. That and the knowledge that everything depended on her. The whole of Amy's future rested on her shoulders because there were no other relatives to fall back on—no conveniently placed grandparents who could help out, no aunts and uncles to tide them over. Leigh had never missed the presence of a family as much as she did now.

It wasn't even as though she had a boyfriend to lean on, someone to give her strength when she felt her own failing. True, there had been someone. Sensitive, moody, artistic Mick, with his long hair tied back into a ponytail and his enviable contempt for the bourgeoisie, but that hadn't lasted. It seemed that he was also allergic to responsibility. The thought of helping her to share the strain of bringing up a young child had been just a little too much like hard work for him. 'I'm a free soul,' he had told her. 'Can't be tied down.' And that had been that. Leigh couldn't think about it, without feeling the sour taste of bitterness in her mouth.

It took her ages to find the club, which was about as far from the Underground as it could be, and as she couldn't afford the luxury of a taxi she had to walk the distance, getting lost several times along the way, despite her *A to Z*.

She was feeling quite frazzled by the time she stood outside the club, which resembled a large Georgianfronted house more than anything else.

Her legs, which had covered the distance on autopilot, now seemed to be nailed to the pavement outside. She literally couldn't move a muscle, couldn't take a step forward. She just stood there, a small, motionless figure amidst a throng of pedestrians, with her hair blowing in every direction as she looked nervously at the edifice.

The cold October air pinched her cheeks, turning them rosy, and made her eyes smart.

It was only when she felt the chill, seeping into her bones, that she took a deep breath and made herself walk forward.

Inside was like stepping into another world. Leigh caught her breath and gazed around her in a disoriented fashion. Everything was so subdued. There was no noise. It was as though the twentieth century was something that was happening outside, something that was abandoned once the doors had closed behind her.

The furnishings were lavish, though faded, with the sort of well-worn elegance she associated with country mansions which had been handed down through the generations.

She looked a little wildly around her, feeling thoroughly out of place in what she was wearing. Her carefully co-ordinated outfit was frankly a joke in a place like this. She raked her fingers through her short hair in a nervous gesture, and then summoned up her courage to start looking for the dining room.

She wasn't allowed to get very far.

A middle-aged man materialised in front of her and asked, pointedly, whether she was a member.

'No, but—'

'This establishment,' he said, eyeing her up and down and clearly finding her wanting, 'is not open to the public. I'm afraid I'm going to have to ask you to leave.' He looked like the sort who disapproved of women in general, having access to the club, members or not. The fact that she was not obviously reduced her to the status of the undeserving. He placed his hand on her elbow and Leigh sprang back angrily.

'Wait just a minute!'

'Now, miss,' the gimlet-eyed man said, his voice hardening, 'I hope I'm not going to have any trouble from you.'

And vice versa, Leigh thought acidly, but she forced herself to remain calm.

'I have an appointment to meet someone here,' she said coolly, bristling as he threw her a dubious look.

'And might I ask whom?'

'A Nicholas Kendall.'

The name was enough to bring about a complete transformation. The man deigned to smile, stiff though the smile was.

'Of course, Miss...?'

'Walker.'

'Miss Walker. Ah. If you would care to follow me, I will show you to Mr Kendall's table.' He set off at a leisurely pace, talking all the while. 'I do apologise if I appeared rude, Miss Walker, but we really cannot be too careful here. In winter, particularly, people have an alarming tendency to try and take refuge in here from the cold. The tourists mistakenly think that it's some kind of up-market restaurant.' *Complete idiots*, his voice implied. 'Others simply try and use it as a bolthole out of the weather.' By 'others' he evidently meant undesirables.

Leigh didn't say anything. She looked around her, taking in the large sitting room areas, all with the same dark furnishings and hushed atmosphere, where businessmen—and a very few businesswomen—sat on comfortable chairs, reading newspapers over lunch or else chatting in library tones. It was, she felt, the sort of place where faces might be recognised—politicians, perhaps, or celebrities of one kind or another. No one so much as glanced in her direction as they walked past. A well bred lack of curiosity.

They went up a flight of stairs past what appeared to be a very large library with leather chairs placed seemingly at random and then entered a formal dining area.

She could feel her stomach going into tight, painful knots as destiny drew closer. She blindly followed her guide, staring straight at his back in a useless attempt to ward off the inevitable, and only refocused when they stopped and she became aware of a man, sitting at a table, in front of her.

'Mr Kendall, this young lady, a Miss Walker, is here to join you for lunch, I believe...?'

What, she thought, would he do if the great and good Mr Kendall shook his head and disclaimed knowledge of any such thing? Would she be hurled out of the place by the scruff of her neck, like someone in a cartoon? Would all these discreet, eminent people rise up in anger at having their private bolthole invaded?

'That's right.' The voice was deep, commanding, and she finally forced her eyes to take in the man on the chair. He was scrutinising her, and making no attempt to disguise the fact. Green eyes, not translucent but the peculiar colour of the unfathomable sea, looked at her unhurriedly. There was no open curiosity but calculated assessment. She had the strangest feeling that she was being committed to memory. It was disconcerting.

'May I fetch you an aperitif?'

Leigh nodded distractedly and said, clearing her throat, 'A mineral water. Please. Sparkling.' She could hear the awkward timbre of her voice and realised how, like her clothes, it betrayed her gaucherie in these surroundings.

'Same for me again, George.' Nicholas Kendall continued to look at her as he spoke and, despite the fact that she had never felt so uncomfortable in her life before, Leigh couldn't seem to tear her eyes away from his face.

She had seen one or two pictures of him when she had been doing her research, grainy newspaper photos which had not prepared her for the immediate impact of his looks.

He had a mesmerising face. As someone who had studied art, she could appreciate the harsh definition of its contours. There was nothing soft or compromising about this face; it held a great deal of strength. It would be a wonderful face to try and capture on canvas but a difficult one because, aside from the physical layout of the features, there was a sense of real power and self-assurance there and that was what held her transfixed.

His hair was dark, almost black, as were his lashes, and contrasted disconcertingly with the inscrutable sea-green of his eyes.

'Do you intend to sit down, Miss Walker?' he asked unsmilingly, 'or do you intend to remain clutching the back of the chair and staring at me?'

His words snapped her back to her senses and she sat in a rush of embarrassed confusion. She could feel her heart pounding under her ribcage, and the sheer enormity of trying to sift out what she was going to say left her tongue-tied.

It didn't help that he offered no encouragement whatsoever. He may well have agreed to meet her—a brief interlude between meetings, judging from his impeccably tailored grey suit—but he wasn't going to make her task easy.

'I'm sorry,' she began, 'to have sprung myself on you like this.' She laughed nervously and fiddled with the stem of her empty wine glass. He neither smiled nor did his expression relax. He merely folded his arms and waited for her to carry on. Leigh felt as though she finally knew what it must have felt like, trying to plead your case before the Spanish Inquisition. She didn't dare meet his eyes.

'I guess you must be a little curious as to why I made contact with you...?' She left that as an unspoken question, hovering in the air between them.

'A little...yes,' he drawled.

Their drinks were brought to them, and Leigh gulped a mouthful of mineral water. Anything to steady her nerves. She wished she had ordered a double whisky on the rocks. She could have bolted it back in one swallow and that would have loosened her up, if nothing else.

There were no menus. George, who looked much more human now that she had proved herself to be no intruder, informed them that there was a choice of roast beef, with all the trimmings, roast lamb, with all the trimmings, or poached salmon.

They both ordered the same thing—the salmon—and as George left them she looked at Nicholas's hard, immutable face with helpless foreboding.

'So,' he said finally, 'are you going to tell me why you contacted me? I'm intrigued, but not so intrigued that I intend to waste my time, trying to drag it out of you bit by reluctant bit.' He swallowed some of his whisky and tonic and surveyed her dispassionately over the rim of the glass.

Leigh wondered what her sister could have seen in this man. Sure, he had a certain style, but he was hardly full of warmth and gaiety, was he? Or maybe, she thought, in the right circumstances he was a bundle of laughs. Then, again, her sister had probably not seen him at all. He had simply been the recipient of her own personal, distressing frame of mind at the time.

'I'm not sure where to start,' Leigh said honestly. She wished that she had never arranged to meet him. She wished, frantically, that she had never found herself in the situation that she had, torn between the devil and the deep blue sea, assured of disaster whatever course she chose to take. In a way she almost wished that her sister had never burdened her with this terrible confidence, although she could understand why she had done it. She had wanted to go with a clear conscience.

'Try the beginning,' he told her abruptly.

'Right. In that case, I have to start around eight years ago.' She lowered her eyes, as though not seeing him might dull the impact of what she had to say. She could feel his attention on her, though, wrapped around her like something tangible and forbidding.

'Majorca, nearly eight years ago. A large, expensive, secluded hotel on the coast.'

Business had been booming then. Order books had been full. She could remember it clearly. Jenny had been married a year at the most and she should have been in the throes of newly wedded bliss, but she had been depressed.

At the time Leigh had questioned her but she hadn't persisted. She had only been a teenager then and her sister's problems had hardly been able to dent the youthful bubble around her. Besides, she'd naïvely assumed that nothing could really be amiss with Jenny—Jenny, who had always been there for her, always looked out for her, the prop which had never wavered ever since their parents had died, leaving them with only each other to turn to.

'Majorca.' Nicholas frowned, and she could see him

trying to dredge up memories from years back. 'I could have been there.' He shrugged noncommittally. 'What's the relevance? If you're going to try and convince me that I met you there, you'd better try again. I've never seen you in my life before, and I never forget a face.'

No, he didn't strike her as the sort of man who ever forgot a face. Who ever forgot anything, come to that.

Their food was served. It was a reprieve from trying to figure out just how she was going to tell her little tale, and Leigh gazed at it, weak with relief for the temporary distraction.

Nicholas Kendall had a strong effect on her, though she didn't quite know what it was. She assumed it was because he represented a type she had never encountered in her life before. Certainly, he was as far removed from her sister's husband as to make you wonder whether they even belonged to the same species.

Roy had been a simple, cheerful man, with the rounded frame of someone who enjoyed his food and drink a bit too much. She had always wondered, in fact, what her sister had ever seen in him. Physically, that was, because Jenny was everything to look at that she, Leigh, had never been. They had been the same height, but there the similarity had ended.

Blonde as opposed to Titian, long, wavy hair as opposed to short and straight, a voluptuous body as opposed to the boyishly slender build which Leigh had long ago discovered did very little to bolster her attractiveness to the opposite sex. In the end she had simply accepted the truth that opposites attract.

Now, though, it was something of a shock to be confronted by the man with whom her sister had had her fated one-night stand.

'I'm still waiting to hear what you have to say, Miss Walker.'

Leigh looked at him and eventually said in a low voice, 'You're quite right, Mr Kendall. We've never met before. But you did meet my sister.' She paused in the face of the difficult task of persuading him of the veracity of the claim. Someone more ordinary might well have remembered the isolated incident with Jenny. This man was not ordinary, however. Would he remember one face, one night, eight years ago amid a sea of doubtless willing women?

The eyes, focused on her, were sharper now, picking up clues and trying to fit the pieces together.

'Jennifer Stewart,' Leigh said in a low voice. 'She looked nothing like me. She was blonde, very extrovert. She was in Majorca for a week, mixing business and pleasure. She had a contract to do the design work for a part of the hotel they were in the process of extending.'

'I had to get out of England, away from Roy. I felt awful, but I just had to think... I was mad, grief-stricken,' she had told Leigh in the hospital, her voice barely audible.

Nicholas Kendall recognised her. Leigh could see it in his eyes. She didn't know whether it had been the description or whether he remembered Jennifer because she had been there on business, but remember her he did. He stiffened very slightly. His eyes, which had been uninviting to begin with, now regarded her coldly, as though suspicious of whatever motive had brought her to this encounter. He was, she thought, waiting to shoot her down in flames.

'Quite an eye-stopper,' he said, looking at her and making comparisons.

'Yes, she was.' She looked him fully in the face. 'Unlike me.'

He didn't deny it. 'I remember her because she seemed driven at the time. A little too full of it. Too much laughter, too much chatter, too much drink. How is she?'

It was a polite question. Jennifer had meant nothing to him. She was a quick gallop down memory lane. How ironic that a passing memory would now rise up from nowhere to alter everything in his life, whatever his reaction to her news might be.

'She died in an automobile accident sixteen months ago,' Leigh said abruptly. She toyed with the food in front of her, eating it half-heartedly and shoving the remainder around her plate the way Amy did with her vegetables.

'You have my sympathy.' He glanced at his watch. 'I still don't understand what all this has to do with me, however.'

'Mr Kendall,' Leigh said slowly, putting down her knife and fork and looking ruefully at the half-finished plate of food. It was delicious food but her appetite had deserted her, if it had ever been there in the first place. 'Are you married?' Magazine and newspaper articles had made no mention of a wife, but who knew how these people operated? Fast-lane lives with open marriages.

Thickly fringed green eyes narrowed on her. 'Why do you ask?'

'Are you?'

'I am not.'

Leigh released her breath. Well, that was one less issue that would have to be navigated. The Lord knew, there were enough obstacles, without that being one of them.

'Just say what you have to say, Miss Walker. I'm getting very tired of playing these word games with you. I have no idea why you're here and, frankly I'm beginning to regret my decision to meet you in the first place. You said in the letter that you had something to tell me. Well, tell me.' He took another glance at his watch. 'I haven't got all day.'

'You slept with my sister, Mr Kendall. One night...'

He leaned forward and the black threat on his face made her draw back sharply. 'Yes, I did, Miss Walker. Two consenting adults. If you're going to try and blackmail me in any way whatsoever you're barking up the wrong tree.'

'I have no intention of blackmailing you, Mr Kendall.' She stared at him with loathing. Just what sort of world did this man move in where blackmail was something that featured on the menu? 'I've come here to break some rather...unexpected news. I've come to tell you that you're a father. You have a seven-year-old daughter. Her name is Amy.'

CHAPTER TWO

'WHAT!' The colour had drained from Nicholas Kendall's face and his body was rigid.

'I know that this must come as a shock to you—' Leigh began, and he cut in swiftly, leaning forward, with his elbows on the table.

'What the hell are you playing at? You breeze in here and have the bare-faced nerve to present me with the most deranged story I've ever heard in my entire life, and then you talk to me about shock. I have no idea what's going on in that head of yours, but you must be certifiable if you think that you can try and hold a virtual stranger to ransom over some fabricated piece of nonsense.'

Leigh couldn't recall ever having felt so intimidated in her life before. His expression conveyed shock, disbelief and, now that his colour had returned, a terrible calm. She was reminded of the calm before a storm.

'It's not fabricated, Mr Kendall.' She leaned forward and her voice was urgent. 'Why should I waste my time, fabricating something like this? Do you think that I haven't got better things to do with my time? I'm not playing at anything. Believe me when I tell you that the very last place I want to be right now is here, breaking this news to you.'

'But you felt that you had to…' His mouth twisted cynically and she flinched. 'You must have taken leave of your senses if you think that I'm going to fall for the oldest con trick in the world.' He sat back, but there was nothing relaxed about his posture. Even though he had drawn away from her she still felt as intimidated as when his body had been thrust forward, menacing her.

'Con trick…?' She looked at him in bewilderment.

'And don't play the innocent with me. I'm not sure what you and your sister have cooked up between you, but you're crazy to think that I'm idiot enough to believe a word of what you're saying. You must have thought you'd hit jackpot when I agreed to having remembered your sister. What I don't understand is why she sent you on her behalf. Did she think that your fresh-faced, only-just-out-of-high-school look might have had a bit more sway?'

'I told you, Mr Kendall, my sister was killed in a car accident almost a year and a half ago. And this isn't some kind of con trick. You think that I *want* to be here? What kind of person do you imagine that I am?'

'Presumably one like your sister, Miss Walker.'

'And what exactly is that supposed to mean?'

'Why don't you try working it out for yourself?' he answered in a smooth, soft, menacing voice.

'Nothing you're saying makes any sense. I came here—'

'Having cooked up a plot with your sister—'

'Having done nothing of the sort!' Every instinct in Leigh urged her to get up and leave, but however angry and insulted she was she knew that she could obey none of those instincts. She was utterly trapped—condemned, at least, to conclude what she had begun.

'Get it through your head, Mr Kendall…' she glared at him with loathing '…that egotistical, arrogant head of yours, that I'm not here on some harebrained scheme dreamt up by anyone…'

'Just a courtesy call to let me know that I'm a father...' His eyes narrowed to slits, and she half expected him to stand up and inform her that he had had enough of her time-wasting. She knew that if he did that, if he walked out on her now, then her audience with him was gone for ever.

'No, of course this isn't a courtesy call!' She felt a sense of hopeless misery, welling up inside her. Her hands were clenched into tight fists.

'Which really only leaves us one other possibility—wouldn't you agree, Miss Walker?'

She looked at him and felt once more at the mercy of an overwhelming personality. This, she reckoned, was the last place in the world she would choose to be. Shark-infested waters would be preferable.

'I'm *not* trying to con you, Mr Kendall,' she said stubbornly, miserably.

'I dislike stupidity, Miss Walker. I dislike it even more when people try and camouflage it with guile.' He regarded her coldly and she met his wintry eyes with a sudden rush of hot, giddy anger.

'This was a mistake,' she muttered. 'I don't know what possessed me to come here.' She stood up, realising that her legs were unsteady.

'Sit down!'

'Go to hell!' She began to walk away. Her whole body was hot and trembling. She needed to get some cool air on her face. In a minute she would combust—at least, that was how she felt. She was hardly aware of him behind her until she felt his fingers around her arm, slowing her down.

'Take your hands off me,' she snarled through gritted teeth, 'or I'll scream my head off loud enough to have all these stuffed people in here running for cover.'

Something flickered in his eyes—she couldn't tell what—and he removed his hand.

'I'm not through with you yet, Miss Walker. Your little plan may have backfired and you may well want to beat a tactical retreat now but you can forget it. You started this and you'll damn well finish it, and I may as well warn you that blackmail is a crime.'

'Don't you threaten me!' She stared at him in wide-eyed horror. Crime? What was he talking about? She hadn't done anything wrong but she felt like a criminal.

'Oh, dear, losing your grip on the proceedings?' He gave a short, acid laugh.

'You're mad,' she said flatly. 'Completely mad. You can believe what you like about my motives for being here, but if you have no intention of hearing me out I certainly don't intend to stay here while you have fun, pulling me to shreds.' She met his eyes, without blinking.

He didn't answer. He stared back at her in silence and she knew that he was working out whether to give her a chance to say what she had come to say, even if it confirmed every accusation he had levelled against her, or whether to have her thrown out and put the whole thing down to an unpleasant episode with a crackpot.

'We'll talk in one of the sitting rooms,' he said grimly. 'I'm prepared to listen to what you have to say but, so help me, if this is a ploy to get money out of me I'll personally see to it that you regret the day you—'

'Are you accusing me of gold-digging?' Leigh whispered, trying hard to feel relief and gratitude instead of sheer fury at his assaults.

They were walking through another part of the building, towards what she now saw was yet another sitting area, though not one of those she had passed on the way in. Its only occupant was a man who was well into his seventies and was fast asleep with a newspaper open on his lap. The room was furnished in dark reds, heavy colours that brought to mind images of clarets and ports and the savouring of fine wines. There was a very masculine feel to it which was daunting though not entirely unpleasant.

They sat in chairs furthest away from the sleeping man, facing one another like combatants. Which, she considered bleakly, was what they were.

'I'm an extremely wealthy man, Miss Walker. It does tend to instil a certain amount of cynicism.'

Leigh didn't say anything. She was here, she knew, for help. True, she had not come voluntarily, but because she had found herself in a corner from which all other routes seemed barred. But wasn't she appealing for some kind of financial assistance when all was said and done? It was a humiliating situation in which to find herself, particularly because Nicholas Kendall had no intention of letting her off the hook with pleasantries. He was accommodating her now, but only because he was curious.

'I suppose so,' she admitted reluctantly, linking her fingers together on her lap.

'You *suppose* so?'

'Yes, well, I really have no experience of... I've never mixed in circles...' She had no real idea what he'd meant when he'd said that he was extremely wealthy but she was beginning to get an idea. It was there in the deference of George, in his self-assurance, which spoke of someone accustomed to giving orders and having them obeyed, and in the cut of his clothes.

It was stamped on him so clearly that he might just as well have been carrying a sign on his forehead. A ready target for gold-diggers, she assumed. More so because of his compelling good looks.

Not many men had such a combination. The thought of anyone cultivating someone else because of the size of their bank balance was something she found so distasteful, however, that she could barely get her mind around it.

Another elderly man, who bore a striking resemblance to George and treated Nicholas in the same deferential manner, took an order for two coffees. As soon as he had left, Nicholas leaned forward and said bluntly, 'So you're telling me that I went to Majorca eight years ago, spent one night with your sister and I am the father of a seven-year-old child as a result.'

Leigh nodded.

'And if all that is true, which I don't for a minute concede it is, why have you only now come to me with this information? Why didn't your sister tell me about the pregnancy? She knew my name, she could have tracked me down without a great deal of difficulty. I'm well known in financial circles.'

'It's a long story,' Leigh replied nervously.

'I'm all ears.' He sat back, crossed his legs and regarded her with those bottomless green eyes. 'I'm eager to know why you would suddenly decide that my paternal rights might count for something.'

He might be sitting here, she thought, he might have told her that he was prepared to hear what she had to say, but she could tell from the look on his face that he was less prepared to believe what he might hear.

'My sister was married at the time you met her,' Leigh began slowly, and his eyebrows shot up.

'Really? Well, she certainly kept quiet about that.'

'She would have been wearing a wedding ring,' Leigh pointed out, and he shrugged.

'I don't automatically look at a woman's finger when she's in the process of throwing herself at me.'

'Oh, I see. You just take what's on offer.'

'Before you start questioning my morals, I'd advise you to look a little more closely at your sister's, Miss Walker.'

He made it sound as though Jenny had been nothing more than a common tramp, and Leigh clamped down on the temptation to launch into a vitriolic defence of her sister's state of mind at the time.

Jenny had been no tramp, she knew that. She had thrown herself into her night of insanity with the abandon of someone trying to forget the present, drowning her sorrow in a single act whose repercussions she could never have foreseen.

'Jenny had her reasons for her behaviour, Mr Kendall,' she said coldly. 'What were yours?'

He didn't like that. His face darkened. 'I don't suppose you've come here to debate my morals, Miss Walker, but if it's of any interest to you I tried to get in touch with her the following morning, only to find that she had checked out.'

'And what a blow that must have been to you.'

'No one speaks to me like that!'

'I can speak to you any way I please.' She couldn't, she knew, but wisdom was trailing very far behind a reckless desire to speak her mind, whatever the consequences. She refused to be cowed by his money and power.

'I don't fool around with married women.'

Leigh shrugged, abandoning the impulse to give him a lecture on Men Of His Type. What was the point? He said that he didn't fool around with married women. What was to be gained by debating the issue? Besides, maybe he was telling the truth, maybe he was loaded with moral virtue, maybe principles were coming out of his ears. If that were the case, then it was unfortunate for him that his looks seemed to tell a different story.

'Well,' she continued, 'whatever. Your principles are your business and they have nothing to do with why I'm here.' He looked as though he wanted to shake her into agreeing with him, and she ignored the look on his face. 'Jenny was married at the time and...' she scoured her brain for the right way of saying what she was about to say '...things weren't going too well. Or, rather, they were going very well, but—'

'Perhaps you could get your facts straight...'

'I would if you'd give me half a chance!' She glared at him, pausing while George's clone sidled towards their table and deposited a tray with percolated coffee, cups, saucers, sugar and milk.

'She had just had some bad news,' Leigh hissed, leaning forward and sloshing coffee and milk into her cup. Let him pour his own. If he found it so difficult to be civil to her she was damned if she was going to make an effort to show any civility towards him. This whole meeting was turning out to be a full-blown disaster, anyway.

'Odd way to react to bad news, don't you think?' He poured his coffee—no milk—and sat back in the chair and regarded her coldly. 'Leaving the country for a jaunt in a foreign hotel away from hearth and home and, now you tell me, husband.'

'You don't understand...'

'If she was that blissfully married why didn't she talk out with her husband whatever problems she was having? You haven't exactly thought out this story logically, have you, Miss Walker? Or did you think that I'd fall for whatever you said to me, hook, line and sinker, with no questions asked?'

Two bright patches of colour appeared on her cheeks, and Leigh swallowed back the renewed temptation to storm out of the club.

'Look, Mr Kendall,' she said evenly, 'I realise that you think yourself the world's most eligible bachelor. You seem to think that no woman could possibly approach you unless her intentions were devious, which, incidentally, is a very sad state of affairs, but I assure you that I haven't lain in bed, plotting and planning this meeting. I'm here because I've found myself in the position of having no other option.'

'World's most eligible bachelor...' He linked his fingers together and a half-smile crossed his darkly cynical face, though not quite reaching his eyes which remained cool and shrewd. 'Oh, I don't think so.' His eyes caught hers and held them fractionally too long for Leigh's comfort.

'No,' she said politely, 'I don't think so either. Anyway, if I might be allowed to continue?'

'Carry on.'

'You have to understand that all of this...everything that I'm telling you now... I knew nothing about all this at the time. I only found out...' She hated talking about Jenny, about the accident. At the time she had had to be brave for Amy's sake, but the awful reality of it had been only a heartbeat away. Time made it easier to accept, but right now she felt that if she dwelt too hard on her sister's death she would find herself giving in to the temptation to bawl her eyes out.

She didn't imagine that the man sitting opposite her would appreciate the outburst of emotion.

'She and Roy—that was her husband—'

'Who was also involved in this so-called accident—'

'That's right, and there's nothing "so-called" about it.'

'What happened?'

'Does it matter?'

'Was she your only sibling?'

Leigh looked at him with frustration. Why wouldn't he just let her finish her piece? Having jumped down her throat, why was he now dragging this information out of her? She didn't like talking about it. In fact, she seldom did. She had wept at the funeral, but her thoughts she preferred to keep to herself. Circumstances had hardened her, forced her to become self-reliant.

'Yes,' she answered abruptly.

'What about other relatives? Aunts, uncles? You haven't mentioned your parents so I assume that they're no longer on the scene.'

'This is irrelevant,' Leigh told him brusquely. 'If I'd known you'd ask all these questions I would have come armed with a family tree.'

Nicholas looked at her carefully. 'Why do you say that coming to me was the last resort? If there were relatives around, I assume—'

'That I would have rushed to them for help first. Of course.' Silly of me to assume that he might have been showing some kind of personal interest in her and, indirectly, in Amy. 'There's no one else, Mr Kendall. Jenny was all I had.' Saying it out loud made it sound bleak and lonely. She remembered how it had been when her parents had died. She remembered that lost, exposed feeling, but she had been so much younger then and there had been Jenny to hold her hand and help her through. Now there was no one to shield her from the loneliness, waiting to strike.

'Our parents passed away when I was twelve within months of one another. As for relatives, I think there's an uncle somewhere in Australia and my father had a couple of cousins in Canada, but we never kept in touch. Is that sufficient background history, or would you like to know more? Maybe I could throw in my blood group for good measure?' She was annoyed with him for prising information out of her which she had grown accustomed to keeping to herself.

'To cut a long story short, there was no one else to turn to. And, anyway…' She halted, unsure of what to say next.

'And anyway?'

'I happen to think that it's important for Amy to eventually know who her father is,' Leigh told him defiantly. 'Even if it's an intrusion on your lifestyle.'

'Let's just suppose that I give you the benefit of the doubt for a minute, that I actually believe what you're telling me, don't you find it a bit odd that you only suddenly thought it important nearly a year and a half after the event?'

'She's only seven…'

'You were waiting until?'

She looked at him with deep dislike. Did he believe a word of what she was saying? Was he simply humouring her? Allowing her to have her say until his coffee was finished, whereupon he would coolly look her up and down and tell her to be on her way? She couldn't even tell whether she was getting through to him at all because, whatever he said, his face remained unreadable.

'Until she was a bit older.' Leigh took a mouthful of

her coffee, which was now tepid and quite disgusting. 'Until she was more capable of...understanding...'

'Thoughtful of you.'

What would it feel like to throw her tepid coffee all over him? she wondered. Would it wipe that expression of cynical self-assurance off his face?

'Why did you say that you were willing to hear what I've got to say, Mr Kendall? You don't want to hear a word I've got to say. You want to dig a hole, chuck me in, cover me with earth and then walk away, wiping your hands.'

'What did your sister tell you?'

'You were right,' Leigh said eventually. 'She was driven when you met her in Majorca. Not herself. I knew at the time. I vaguely recall that she was miserable, but she didn't confide in me. I guess she had always been in the role of my protector so she felt that she had to protect me even from her own unhappiness. It turns out that...' She sighed and ran her fingers through her short hair so that any attempt at neatness was instantly lost.

'She and Roy had been trying for a family. Before they were married, even. Apparently. I knew nothing about all of this. The week before she had been to the doctor for the results of tests. It turned out that there was a problem. Roy couldn't father a child. Jenny was devastated. Having children meant everything to her. In hospital she told me that she had even started buying pregnancy magazines in anticipation of the large family she and Roy were going to have.'

'Are you trying to tell me that she went on holiday with the express purpose of mating with a suitable specimen?' His mouth twisted cruelly, and Leigh shot him a helpless look from under her lashes.

'Are you hearing what I'm saying? She was desperately unhappy when she went on that one-week break. She needed to be away from Roy, needed to think, but the more she thought the more unhappy she became, and for the first time in her life she did something totally out of character for her. She had a one-night stand.

'As luck would have it, she got pregnant and decided to keep Amy. She said that she and Roy discussed it. They went through a rough patch for a while but he loved her and in the end he accepted the circumstances. He loved Amy as though she were his own.' She drew a deep breath. 'Look, I'm sorry that man was you. I'm sorry that you've had all this foisted onto you. It must be a nightmare. It's also a fact of life.'

'Why do you think that I would believe a word of what you're telling me?' He looked at her coolly, assessingly, without a hint of emotion on his face.

'Because it happens to be the truth.'

'And now are you going to tell me why you've been overwhelmed by the sudden desire to fill me in?'

Temporary insanity, Leigh thought, staring at her coffee-cup, a moment of sheer madness. Frankly, you're the last person in the world I would want to confront with this dilemma.

'Because circumstances have changed, Mr Kendall,' she said awkwardly.

'In other words, you're broke. I wondered when we would arrive at the financial angle. Never mind the ethics of letting me know of this mysterious daughter's existence.'

He nodded imperceptibly in the direction of the door, and George wafted into the room to remove their cups and saucers. The sleeping man in the armchair was beginning to stir. Leigh could feel Nicholas drawing away from her, signalling the end of her allotted time, and she

was filled with a sudden, panicky desperation. As far as
he was concerned, it all boiled down to money in the
end after all.

'You have a daughter, Mr Kendall, like it or not. You
can pretend to yourself that I'm nothing more than a
cheap gold-digger and you can walk out of here and
never look back, but that won't change the fact that you
fathered a child. I hope that knowledge burns a hole in
your conscience for the rest of your life.' Damn him if
he thought that he would simply walk away and forget
every word she'd said. Things were crashing down
around her. She had swallowed quite a mouthful of hum-
ble pie, coming to this man. She would make sure that
he knew it.

'Don't moralise to me, Miss Walker.'

'I'll damn well do as I please, Mr Kendall.' She
leaned forward and urgency lent her a desperate sort of
courage. 'Roy and Jenny left behind them a cartload of
debt. I've spent the past few months lying awake every
night, worrying about where the money was going to
come from. I've struggled in a job that barely pays, I've
struggled to be the emotional support system my niece
needs and I feel as though I've worn myself to the bone.

'I've come to you, yes, for help because I have nowhere else to go. The bank has foreclosed on the house.
I don't care about me, but there's Amy to consider. She's
a child. She's *your* child!' She was trembling and every
nerve in her body felt stretched to breaking point. She
no longer cared what sort of impression she made. If she
had to crawl on all fours she would do it, provided it
went some way to ensuring some kind of future for
Amy.

It occurred to her that there might be someone in the

room who had overheard her, and she looked around surreptitiously.

'No need,' he told her, with less hostility in his voice than she would have expected. 'That's the beauty of this place. No one pays the slightest bit of attention to other people's conversations. Even if something sensitive was screamed out to all four corners you would still be guaranteed that it would remain within these walls.' He paused. 'Not that I give a jot what opinion the rest of the world has of me.'

'That must give you a great sense of freedom,' Leigh said, distracted as much by what he had said as by his unruffled response to her slightly raised voice.

He looked at her curiously, as though trying to weigh her up.

'You'll understand that I will want a blood test to establish paternity.'

'So you do agree that it's possible that I'm telling you the truth. That I'm not some avid little gold-digger who's shown up on your doorstep eager to see what I can cream off you.'

'All things are possible.' He shrugged.

'You can have a million blood tests. They'll back me up.' She smiled for the first time, a secret, amused smile, and he frowned as though she had suddenly retreated to a place from which he was excluded.

'But...?' he asked, frowning.

'But nothing...' But, she thought, you won't need one. His physical resemblance to Amy was almost scary. 'Will you just meet her, Mr Kendall? If you choose to wash your hands of the whole matter after that, then so be it.'

She heard the supplication in her voice with mortification. It was true that she would have told Amy about her natural father in time, and would have supported her in whatever choice she made as to whether to seek him out or not. But to be reduced to presenting this man with this dilemma, forced to beg, made her cringe.

'I'll meet...the child,' he said heavily.

'When?'

'The sooner the better, I suppose.' He rose, and as Leigh joined him she was aware, more forcibly this time, of his height, his muscularity, the way he towered over her and made her feel small, even though she was a respectable enough height.

'I would appreciate it,' she said, following him out of the building into the bracing cold outside, 'if you could—'

'Not let the child know my relationship to her?'

Leigh nodded and pulled her jacket tightly around her. The wind whipped her skirt around her legs like clambering vines. She would have been more comfortable in her usual out-of-work attire of jeans.

'I think we should wait and see what develops from here,' he said, looking down at her.

He wasn't, she realised, about to assume anything. This potentially life-changing situation with which he had been confronted did not exist, as far as he was concerned, until it was proven.

'When would you like me to introduce you to her?' Leigh asked shortly.

'What about the weekend? Sunday. I'll meet you for lunch somewhere. Where do children of that age like to eat?' It sounded as though children were a species foreign to him.

'Any fast-food chain,' she told him quickly, before he could change his mind, and he frowned, as though trying to identify the name of a fast-food chain. *Any* fast-food chain.

'Conversation might be a little difficult in one of those places. I know a hamburger restaurant in the Covent Garden area. I believe they serve all the usual child-friendly things, milkshakes and ice cream. She does eat…stuff like that, doesn't she?'

'Adores it.' Leigh smiled.

'And who should I introduce myself as? Old friend of the family?' His mouth twisted. 'Distant relative?'

'I'll tell her that you're a friend.' Thank heavens, Leigh thought, that she's only seven. Much older than that and she would be hard pressed to believe that Nicholas Kendall could be anything but a relative, so perfectly did his face mirror hers.

'Fine.' He continued to look at her. 'And don't forget what I said,' he murmured with a warning in his voice, bending slightly so that his breath was on her face, warm and disorienting. 'I'm no fool. Child or no child, I won't be taken for a ride.'

'I wouldn't dream of it, Mr Kendall.'

'Nicholas.'

'I beg your pardon?'

'Nicholas. You might just as well call me by my first name. Mr Kendall might just be a little formal, considering I'm a long-lost family friend.' He glanced at his watch, quickly reeled off the name of the restaurant he had in mind and the address, and with mixed feelings Leigh watched him depart in long, easy strides.

Step one, at any rate, had been accomplished. The only problem was that she had no idea what step two would entail.

She turned on her heel and on the journey back to the house she tried to work out what the options were because, whether he knew it or not, he would have no difficulty in accepting that Amy was his.

Money, of course, was the issue. She could repay him as much as she could month by month—a bit like taking out a loan with the bank. She didn't need much to look after Amy. They would have to find a roof over their heads, something small and sensible. It hardly mattered whether it was in a fashionable district or not, just so long as wherever they lived was safe. She might at least be granted the breathing space to look for a better job, something that would make her more financially solvent.

His contribution, if he decided to help, would be a drop in the ocean to him, no doubt about it, but it could be the lifeline she and Amy so desperately needed.

It was only as she was letting herself into the house that a thought suddenly occurred to her. A very unpleasant thought. What if he decided to fight for custody of his daughter? He was wealthy and powerful, a man with quite a few guns in his armoury. What if he took one look at his offspring and decided that he would plunge into fatherhood, having been denied it for seven years?

Leigh removed her jacket and made herself a cup of tea, her body on autopilot as her mind wrestled this unforeseen possibility.

No, she told herself. Look at things in a logical manner. Nicholas Kendall was not married. He had no experience of children and, from what she had seen, he was probably the last man on the face of the earth to *want* any experience of them.

She had no real idea what he did for a living but, whatever it was, it doubtless ate up his time. People rarely acquired huge sums of money working in part-time jobs. No, he was probably one of those odious men who lived for their work. He probably rented a bachelor penthouse suite somewhere in Belgravia, an exquisite two-bedroom affair with a daily cleaning service. The sort of place where children and pets were banned.

I can't let myself get embroiled in complications before they arise, she told herself. I can't think ahead beyond what happens at the next meeting. I can't let myself.

I just have to think of Amy.

CHAPTER THREE

'I DON'T want to wear a dress.' Amy looked at the blue and white polka-dotted dress neatly laid out on the bed and folded her arms.

'It's a lovely dress, Ames.' Leigh was reduced to pleading.

'I want to wear my jeans and a jumper.'

'But that's what you stay around the house in!'

'We're only going out for a burger,' Amy said, with a little too much logic for Leigh's liking. '*No one* dresses up for a burger.' There had been a time when she would willingly have donned any item of clothing Leigh put in front of her, but recently she had developed strong preferences, something Leigh had found charming, the sign of a strong and independent mind. Until now. Now she just wanted Amy to look *right*, like the beautiful little girl that she was.

'Anyway,' Amy said stubbornly. 'I'm much too old for that dress.'

'It's a very pretty dress.' Leigh could sense defeat in the air and she waved the dress around despairingly. 'OK, a compromise. You can wear the jeans but not that jumper. You can wear the jeans with the orange jumper.'

Amy looked as though she would throw that out as well, but eventually she nodded. 'And my lace-up boots?'

'Why not?'

Did all mothers have to go through this? Leigh wondered. Parental responsibility had been thrust on her, and

44

now she wished she had paid closer attention to how Jenny had handled her daughter. She vaguely recalled that the strict approach had not been used, but would she have given in in these circumstances?

She remained where she was, kneeling on the floor, while her niece got into her jeans, a blue denim polo shirt and the orange jumper, and decided that Amy looked very fetching after all. Not quite *The Little House on the Prairie* style, but cute. Cute and trendy. And Nicholas Kendall would probably have no one to compare her to, anyway. She doubted if he knew anyone under four feet and ten years of age.

'Hat?' Amy asked, pulling out a black, fake-fur-lined number from the darkest corners of her wardrobe. Leigh shrugged and nodded and gave up the battle completely.

'You look sweet,' she said, rising to her feet then almost falling over again because of the sudden attack of pins and needles in her legs. She stamped her feet to get rid of them.

'Thanks.' Amy smiled and made a face which was supposed to resemble sweet but looked more like a grimace. 'Your friend must be someone special,' she said. 'You're wearing a skirt again.'

'He's not *my* friend,' Leigh said hastily, glancing in the mirror and deciding that 'sweet' was probably the best she could hope for as well in her swinging green and brown skirt and her baggy brown jumper. She had tried to add on a few years by sticking on a string of pearls, her only concession to jewellery, but she still only managed to look like a teenager. 'He used to know your mum,' she said, playing with the truth rather than resorting to an out and out lie.

Amy didn't say anything. She was getting better when it came to any mention of Jenny. For months her eyes had filled up when her mother had been mentioned, but now the present was gradually forming its own layers over memories of the past. Children were resilient, Leigh had been told at the time. In many ways they handled grief far better than adults because they never tried to hide their mourning or to put on a brave face.

'She never mentioned him to me,' Amy said, following Leigh out of the bedroom and conversing with her back.

She could be surprisingly grown-up in some of her responses. Leigh supposed that was a function of being an only child.

'Maybe she did and you forgot,' Leigh answered, without turning around. 'It doesn't matter anyway. It was very nice of him to ask us out.' *Nice?* Ha. If only. Nicholas Kendall couldn't be *nice* if he spent ten years studying it at university.

They went to Covent Garden on the Underground, and reached the restaurant with time to spare. It was busy. The background music was loud, and people seemed to be on the move constantly—waiters and waitresses with huge trays, which they held expertly with one hand, people coming and going and generally paying no heed to the idea that Sunday was a day of rest.

Leigh ordered soft drinks for both of them and then proceeded to take very small sips from hers, working on the theory that there was no point letting him see a nearly finished glass and assuming that she had rushed over with Amy, desperate and eager.

Her stomach hurt. She could feel the tension curling and uncurling in it, and even though she made a tremendous effort to focus all her attention on Amy her eyes drifted relentlessly to the door of the restaurant, watching and waiting and watching and waiting.

So she was surprised when she took a sip of her drink, bent to rescue Amy's napkin from the floor and straightened to find him standing right there in front of their table.

Amy was looking at him with blatant curiosity and he was staring back at her.

He was transfixed. Leigh could see it on his face. And she could also see why. Together, like this, the physical resemblance between them was even more striking than she had expected.

They both had precisely the same shade of hair, precisely the same colour and shape of eye, the same shaped mouth. Even their expressions seemed to mirror one another. It was uncanny.

'Hi!' Leigh broke the silence and Nicholas dragged his eyes away from his daughter and sat down. 'Nice to see you, Nicholas!' She hoped she sounded like someone greeting an old friend of the family, instead of a stranger greeting a possible threat to her well-being. 'Nicholas, I'd like you to meet my niece, Amy.'

'It's nice to meet you, Amy,' he said a little awkwardly. 'I've brought you a little present.' He reached into his trouser pocket and took out a small parcel. 'I was sorry to learn about what happened to your...your parents.'

'What is it?' Amy neither acknowledged his condolences nor did she make any move to take the gift. After a while she looked at Leigh, asking permission with her eyes, and when Leigh nodded she took the box tentatively, as though fearful that contact with this stranger's hand might result in third-degree burns. Leigh could sympathise with the sentiment.

'Just a little something I picked up.' Nicholas looked at Leigh and his expression was controlled, though she couldn't see behind the veneer to the man beneath. Was he angry? Taken aback? Finally shocked at the proof of his one-night stand in the chair opposite him, carefully unwrapping the present?

Amy opened the lid of the box and withdrew a gold charm bracelet from inside, which she turned over and over.

'May I keep it?'

'I guess.'

'Of course you can. It's a present.'

They answered at the same time and Leigh shot him a polite warning from under her lashes. Amy's father he might well be, but this was a delicate situation, to be handled very carefully one step at a time. Barging his way in and assuming rights was not going to work, and she intended to make that very clear from the outset. Why had he come bearing gifts, anyway? she thought a little resentfully. This was supposed to be a first meeting, not an extravaganza of buying affection.

The meal was a long, awkward business. Nicholas did his best to chat to Amy, who replied in uninformative monosyllables, bemused by the garrulousness of a man she had never laid eyes on in her life before.

Every so often she opened the box with the bracelet, and looked at the sliver of gold coiled in the bottom.

And, thought Leigh, I'm hardly any better at defusing the tension of the situation. Old family friends should have had a few anecdotes to fall back on but, of course, there was no such easy escape route for her so she had to strive uncomfortably between sounding way too hearty and downright ill at ease. It was a finely balanced act, made all the more difficult since Amy was an observant child, quick to spot nuances.

Still, it was with some trepidation when, after the meal

was finished, Amy announced that she needed to go to the toilet.

'I can find it myself,' she said, as Leigh began to rise to her feet.

'Are you sure?'

'It's downstairs. I came here ages ago with Mum and Dad.'

An uncomfortable silence greeted this remark, which Amy, thankfully, didn't notice. Leigh smiled and ignored the observation, but she didn't look at Nicholas. She had spent the past hour and a half trying to read the expression on his face and failing. She just knew—some process of instinct at work—that he had not been terribly impressed either with her or with the situation. Maybe both. He certainly gave no inclination of being anything but interested in his daughter.

'So…' Leigh said, attempting to establish some control over the proceedings by speaking first, 'your daughter… Now, I recall you said something about a paternity test—'

'You know damn well that there will be no paternity test. The child—'

'Is the image of you.' Leigh finished on his behalf.

'And that gives you a sense of satisfaction?' he said through gritted teeth. 'What the hell gave your sister the right to do what she did? To find herself pregnant and then play God with someone else's child's future?' He leaned forward, an aggressive movement which had Leigh flinching back into her seat.

'We've been through all this,' she said warily, eyeing him the way a zoologist might have eyed a new and potentially dangerous species of animal.

'Well, we'll damn well go through it again!' He banged his closed fist on the table and it was almost a shocking physical display of the hostility behind his words. Now that Amy wasn't present there was no need for him to maintain any semblance of politeness, and the speed with which he shed it was frightening.

Now Leigh could see what it was that had been bothering her from the start. It was his thinly disguised rage.

'She only did what she thought was best at the time,' Leigh answered, leaning forward and refusing to be cowed by this display of menacing emotion. 'She hadn't anticipated getting pregnant—'

'But she did!'

'Yes, I know, but—'

'But you're obliged to stand up for her, aren't you?' he said with scathing disgust. 'Heaven only knows, you probably think along precisely the same lines. After all, you both come from the same mould, don't you?'

'That's not fair. How dare you!' She clasped her fingers together and waited, trembling, for the rush of blood to her head to ebb.

'Your sister had my child and had no intention of ever letting me find out that I was a father.'

There was no point denying the truth behind that and Leigh didn't bother to try. In a way she could understand why her sister had acted the way she had. However, in another way she could see the injustice of it and in the long term the possibility of a great deal of complications. It was one of those situations which seemed to preclude a good outcome for all involved. Somewhere along the line someone was going to get hurt.

'Amy would have found you sooner or later,' she said, doing her very best to understand what he must be going through. 'And it's pointless to continue arguing about this—'

'And you had the cheek to examine my ethics in sleeping with your sister!'

Out of the corner of her eye Leigh saw Amy climbing up the steps and she plastered a smile on her face, even though the effort of it made her jaw ache.

'May I have some dessert?' she asked, as soon as she had sat down at the table. 'I saw a banana split downstairs and it looked yummy.' She slurped some of her drink noisily through the straw and eyed her aunt from under her dark lashes, the same lashes that fringed her father's eyes. How was it that she couldn't see her startling resemblance to the man sitting next to her? But, then, children often failed to notice the most glaring things.

'I really think that it's time for us to go now, Ames.' Leigh scrunched her paper napkin up in a meaningful way and glanced around for a waiter. 'You haven't done your homework yet.'

'It's just maths,' Amy said.

'You like maths, do you?' Nicholas asked, concealing his brooding anger with difficulty, and Amy bestowed on him one of those indulgent, faintly superior looks that children were wont to give adults who were trying their hardest to make conversation.

'I'm good at it.' She shrugged, thought a bit, then continued, 'Mum and Dad used to say that I was better than them.'

'I was very good at the sciences as well,' Nicholas said conversationally, his eyes hooded. 'Comes in useful in later life.'

Amy appeared not to quite follow what he was getting at. 'You mean, looking for a job?' she asked, frowning and draining her glass of the very dregs of her drink.

'That's right, though I don't suppose you've given much thought to what you want to do when you grow up.'

'I want to be a ballerina,' she said, after a while.

'That sounds…interesting,' Nicholas said, at a loss for words.

'Do you know any ballerinas?'

'Can't say that I do. But we could perhaps go to a ballet one of these days.'

'Could we?' Amy's eyes lit up momentarily like a Christmas tree.

'Maybe,' Leigh said stiffly, feeling like a stick in the mud and resenting having been placed in the position of sounding like one.

'The *Nutcracker* usually comes around Christmas time.'

'We'll see,' Leigh pressed on sharply, and Nicholas met her eyes with steely determination.

'Do you have a problem with me taking Amy out somewhere?'

'Oh, no, not at all…'

'I'm glad to hear it.'

'It's just that Christmas is such a busy time…'

'But, Aunty Leigh…'

'Anyway, it's time for us to go.' Leigh looked around desperately for a waiter and signalled to the first one she saw.

'Perhaps,' Nicholas said to Amy, reaching into his pocket for his wallet, 'you could spare your aunt for a short while when we get back. Have you any friends you could spend an hour or two with? There are one or two things I need to talk to her about.'

'I'm sitting right here,' Leigh said coldly, dropping the happy, smiling mask. 'Kindly leave Amy out of it.'

Amy was beginning to look confused at this turn of events. She glanced from one to the other and then took refuge in playing with the box containing the bracelet.

'We need to have a little chat.' His voice contained a quiet, disturbing edge to it that started off a little nervous reaction in her stomach. She wasn't accustomed to dealing with men like this. His eyes held hers and she had a sudden sensation of complete disorientation.

'Of course,' she said, 'but we could arrange—'

'Sooner rather than later…'

'Yes, but it's terribly difficult to find someone to babysit Amy at such short notice…'

'I could go and play with Sophie,' Amy volunteered, pleased with herself for having found a solution to the problem.

'Sophie might be busy on a Sunday afternoon,' Leigh pointed out.

'Perhaps we could try anyway,' Nicholas said softly. 'Is this a neighbour? I'll take you both there in my car.'

Leigh nodded and watched with a sinking feeling as he settled the bill and stood up. He was taking over. She supposed, when she thought about it, that it was to be expected, but she realised that the possibility had never really crossed her mind.

She had, she now saw, been unbelievably naïve. She had wanted help and had been vaguely pleased that she was doing the right thing, in telling Nicholas Kendall about the existence of his daughter, but she had still assumed that her life would carry on as it had, perhaps with fewer financial headaches.

Naïve or else just plain stupid.

His car was parked on double yellow lines outside the restaurant, and on closer inspection Leigh could see that it hardly mattered since there was a chauffeur behind the wheel. He sprang out as soon as he saw Nicholas, opened the car door so that she could slip into the back seat with Amy and, in the manner of all good chauffeurs, showed an admirable lack of curiosity.

'Where do you live?' Nicholas asked from the front seat, and Leigh leaned forward and told him.

The car eased its way out of Covent Garden like a sleek, jungle animal—a top-of-the-range BMW, deep blue, polished and gleaming. People turned to watch as it drove past. Sitting in the back seat, Leigh felt a complete phoney but Amy was delighted, and peered out of the window with a solemn but pleased expression.

They covered the distance to the house in record time, and while Leigh reluctantly fixed up with Sophie's mother for Amy to pop across for an hour Nicholas remained outside.

It was clear what he had been doing as soon as she re-emerged because the chauffeur was no longer in evidence.

'He's making his own way back to the apartment,' Nicholas said tightly. 'Gives us more flexibility.' His hands were thrust into his pockets and the stiff, cold breeze blew his hair across his face. 'Have you arranged for Amy to go and visit her friend?'

'I'll drop her across now—it's just a couple of houses along.' Leigh hesitated, not quite sure what was to happen next. 'Perhaps it might be easier if you just came in and had a cup of coffee,' she said.

Nicholas nodded curtly and followed her inside the house, looking around him as he entered as though the surroundings were yet more pieces of a jigsaw puzzle that needed to be slotted in.

Amy emerged, clutching two books. She glanced fleetingly at Nicholas and thanked him again for the bracelet as she was leaving the house with Leigh. Turning around to shut the door, Leigh could see that

Nicholas's eyes were fixed on the small figure who had her back to him. Drinking her in.

As she sprinted back, having dropped Amy off, she wondered viciously what she had got herself into.

Had Jenny anticipated this sort of response from her one-night stand? Possibly not. How much could you tell about a person in the space of a few hours, even if you did go to bed with them? Not much. It had been a moment's impulse, but Jenny had never anticipated this sort of situation arising—of that Leigh was quite certain.

Nicholas was standing just where she had left him, and she briskly offered him coffee, aware of him following her into the kitchen and watching as she took the cups from the cupboard and the milk from the fridge.

It was better, she had decided on the way back, to be businesslike about the whole thing. No sentimentality, no dawdling over her sister's motives, no emotional explanations of what had driven her to look him up in the first place.

She handed him his cup and said, without preamble, 'Well, what happens now?'

Nicholas sat at the kitchen table, a solid pine affair, showing the indentations of countless pencils dragged across the surface by Amy as she was growing up. Leigh watched him levelly. She didn't want to indulge in any more speculations as to why Jenny had done what she did.

'I take it that this is the house which is in the process of being repossessed?'

Leigh looked around her and saw the years roll back to better times. 'Yes,' she answered shortly.

'It's charming. It must have been a delightful place for a child to grow up in.'

'Amy was happy, yes,' she said, looking at him over

the rim of the cup and not particularly liking this turn in the conversation. Was it leading somewhere? He didn't strike her as the sort of man who indulged in too many vacuous pleasantries.

'Has the bank given you some sort of deadline?'

Ah, this was more like it.

'Not as such, but I know that it's going to be sooner rather than later. Jen's accountant is sorting through all the financial mumbo-jumbo, and then the house will be sorted out.'

'What had you planned to do?'

'Rent, Mr Kendall...'

'Nicholas.'

'I had planned on coming to see you and perhaps being loaned some money so that I could see my way to getting a roof over our heads, provided, of course, that you were satisfied with...the situation.'

'What a very delicate way of phrasing it.' He met her stare unflinchingly. '"Satisfied" is the last adjective I would have used but, as you said, debate on the subject is beside the point. You have presented me with a *fait accompli* and now we deal with it.'

'I agree.' She looked at him, then lowered her eyes because the sensation of being swept along on a tide was too overpowering to bear.

'What did you intend to do with the money?'

'The money?' She frowned, confused.

'The money you envisaged me handing over.'

'Lending.' She corrected him acidly. 'I never intended to take anything that was given, without paying it back. And I planned to rent somewhere for Amy and myself to live, I suppose.'

'And precisely how did you see me fitting into this

picture?' The cold, green eyes watched her as she reddened.

'Naturally, you can maintain contact with Amy...'

'How generous of you. Define what you mean when you say "maintain contact".'

Leigh's chin tilted defensively. 'If you want the truth, I didn't think that you would be that keen on anything too close. I'm not an idiot. I know that this has been thrust upon you and that you probably have very little experience of children by choice.' She nervously swallowed a mouthful of coffee. 'I know that all this interrupts your lifestyle—'

'You know precisely nothing of my lifestyle so please do me the courtesy of not making any sweeping generalisations.'

Leigh stiffened but chose to ignore the sarcasm in his voice. Instead, she asked in a controlled voice, 'Do you have any experience of children, Mr Kendall? Nicholas?'

'Not very much, though I don't see where the question is leading.'

'I came to you because I was in desperate need of money. I'm not going to bother to hide that because you probably know it already anyway. I'm quite happy to make do on a day-to-day basis but everything changes the minute a child is involved.

'Amy needs looking after. She can't eat whatever, whenever. She has to be clothed. Roy and Jennifer—I had no idea how heavily in debt they were. I guess they thought that they would ride out the recession and come out the other side. But I've tried that, I've tried making a go of what's left of their business, and it's not feasible.' She paused for breath.

He looked at her. 'She's a delightful child.'

'Yes. She is.'

'How damned odd to be referring to my own flesh and blood in such a detached, impersonal manner.' There was frustration and anger in his voice, but when he looked at her some of the hostility had gone, although there was still no warmth there. His eyes were cool and speculative, but less judgmental than they had been earlier.

'I understand that...that it's a difficult situation for you, which is why I want to intrude on your life as little as possible. I'm very sorry about all this.'

'Save the regrets,' he said dismissively. 'Now that I've seen her there's no doubt that Amy is my child and, that being the case, I have no intention of sweeping her under the carpet after I've salved my conscience, by giving you a fistful of money to tide you over.'

'It would just be a loan.' What, she wondered, was he trying to tell her? Something behind his words was making her feel uneasy. She had foreseen some kind of mutually agreeable arrangement over visitation, perhaps in the nature of a friend calling round so that Amy would not suspect anything and would have the necessary time to accustom herself to his presence. It seemed he wanted more.

'Don't be ridiculous.' He shook his head impatiently and then sat forward, resting his hands on the table. 'The money is incidental.' He made a dismissive gesture with one hand.

'What are you trying to say?' Leigh asked, chilled at the suspicion that was taking root at the back of her mind.

'I intend to make her a permanent fixture in my life,' he said bluntly, and Leigh blanched in horror as her worst fears were confirmed.

'Yes, well, naturally she'll be a permanent fixture. I mean, I don't expect you—'

'You don't understand what I'm saying.' His eyes held hers and she felt suddenly sick with apprehension. 'I don't want the role of part-time father. Or part-time father, masquerading as family friend.'

Leigh found that she couldn't say anything. She had a weird, dizzy feeling that seemed to spread up from her toes, engulfing every bone and muscle and pore in her body. She had to sit on her hands to stop herself from trembling violently.

'We can reach some kind of agreement...' she whispered desperately.

What had she gone and done? Why had she ever assumed that Nicholas Kendall would obligingly lend her some money, enough to see her through, and then, still obligingly, vanish out of their lives whence he had come? Or at least semi-vanish. Somewhere safely tucked away in the background.

'You do realise that I am Amy's next of kin,' he continued implacably. Leigh could barely nod her response. If he thought that he was going to manoeuvre Amy, her wonderful, beloved niece, out of her life then he was in for a big surprise. Although, a little voice was telling her, he *was* the father, wasn't he? And he *did* have an awful lot of money, whereas she, as guardian, had none. And money, unfortunately, *did* talk, didn't it?

'She doesn't know you from Adam,' Leigh pointed out weakly, finding her voice at last.

'If I went to court I would be able to present a very powerful argument for getting control of her.'

'The court would be sympathetic to me! Amy has never seen you in her life before today.' Her eyes were beginning to glisten and she took a deep breath to con-

trol her emotions. There was no point breaking down.
What good would that do? He would be the last person
on earth who would sympathise.

'Hardly my fault, as I would be compelled to point
out.'

There was no arguing this point. 'I'd fight you every
step of the way, and in the long run it wouldn't do Amy
any good at all, would it? And *she's* the one who matters, isn't she?'

'My point exactly. Let's face facts here, Leigh. Your
sister had my baby and, whatever her intentions at the
time, she withheld the information from me for nearly
eight years. God knows, if circumstances hadn't turned
out the way they have, I would never have been any the
wiser. You are now Amy's guardian, but you're staring
penury in the face by your own admission. How much
money do you actually have in the bank?'

'I'm not sure,' Leigh said almost inaudibly, hating the
man opposite her with a passion she had not felt herself
capable of. 'Not much.'

'In other words, you need financial assistance, and
that's unlikely to come from a bank when the bank is
currently in the process of repossessing your house.'

Everything Nicholas said sounded so logical that she
had a very vivid picture of what would happen if
Nicholas Kendall decided to fight for his daughter in a
court of law.

'But,' he conceded, leaning back and appearing to
give the matter a great deal of thought, 'you're absolutely right, of course. Amy doesn't know me from
Adam, as you've said, and she *is* the one whose future
happiness has to be considered.'

'Yes!' Leigh sagged with relief that he had come to

his senses, though she was still immensely angry that he had managed to get her into such a state of anxiety.

'Which is why I have a proposition to make to you.'

'What kind of proposition?' Leigh asked cautiously.

'There's no need to look so suspicious,' he told her, which instantly fuelled her suspicions yet further. 'What I'm about to propose makes perfect sense.' He paused for a few seconds, valuable time during which she wondered whether she hadn't just leapt from the frying-pan into the fire.

'Oh, yes...'

'I gather that your job leaves something to be desired. You were forced into it by circumstances. Presumably you had other plans for your life before all this happened.'

'Well, yes. I was studying graphic art. I had anticipated— Well, what's the use telling you all this? Events overtook me.'

'But you'd like to give up your job and pursue the education you were forced to cut short.'

'I prefer not to deal in dreams.'

'You've answered the question. There's no need to expound on the subject.' He pushed his chair back slightly so that he could cross his legs.

'It's sometimes possible to deal in dreams, but it takes money, doesn't it?'

'I hadn't planned on using any of your money for myself!'

'The immediate concern would, however, have been a roof over your head.'

'Immediate and *only* concern,' she amended, resenting his implication that she would have jumped on the bandwagon and allowed him to pay for her as well.

'From my point of view, I have a child and now that

the initial shock has worn off I don't intend to shove my responsibilities into some convenient little compartment. I want her to move into my house with me.'

'What? Have you taken leave of your senses? It's out of the question! I won't have you…snatching Amy away from me!'

'You're overreacting,' he responded, his voice like a whiplash. 'You haven't heard the rest of what I have to say.'

'*I'm* overreacting? You want to take my sister's child away from me and you tell me that I'm overreacting? What do you expect me to do? Smile, offer you a cup of tea and discuss packing arrangements?'

'For God's sake, woman, shut up! And listen!'

Leigh made a furious, inarticulate sound, then sat down and pressed her balled fists against her mouth. Her hands were shaking.

'I'm not going to take Amy away from anyone!'

'Then why did you—?'

'I want you to move in with her. That way, all problems will be solved. You'll have the roof over your head that she needs and financial security. You can continue with your college degree, or whatever it was you were doing before your life was turned upside down, and you can pack in the job.'

'I can't sponge off you.'

'Take it or leave it.' He let the impact of those words settle in. 'I have a Victorian house in Hampstead. The basement is accounted for but there's more than enough space for us all to co-exist, and I won't consider you sponging off me because I intend to employ you.'

'As what?' She asked in a whisper, closing her eyes as his words sank in.

'As a nanny,' he offered cooly. 'And before you argue with my proposal I suggest you consider the alternatives very carefully indeed. Amy is my daughter, and I'll fight for her if I have to. And I never lose a fight.'

CHAPTER FOUR

NICHOLAS had known precisely what he was doing. From every possible angle there was no way that he could lose, and no way that Leigh could refuse his offer.

And that, she reflected two weeks later, had been just the beginning.

During that time he had visited twice, installing himself in Amy's affections by bringing her, Leigh thought acidly, gifts which were guaranteed to dazzle the most hardened of children. He had stayed in the house, casually making small talk with her, but his attentions were all for his daughter. He was determined to win her over and, displaying the sort of instinctive charm which has no age barriers, he was succeeding.

'You can't come here with a gift every time you visit,' Leigh had told him when, for the second time, he had appeared with a present, this time a wildly extravagant set of Barbie dolls, equipped with a better wardrobe than most adults possessed.

'Why not?'

Amy had retired to bed for the evening, exhausted, clutching the three Barbie dolls with their ludicrously dazzling ensembles, and there were just the two of them in the sitting room, Leigh had a teacloth in one hand because she has spent most of the two hours of his visit lurking in the kitchen, ruing the day she had contacted him.

'Because what you're doing is buying her,' she said bluntly, disregarding the cool glint in his eye.

'That's your theory, anyway.'

'It happens to be perfectly true. Give her too much too soon and all that'll happen is that she'll depend on you to give her whatever she wants. When the time comes to instil some discipline she'll bitterly resent it as a form of betrayal.'

'And where do you get your child psychology from?'

'From experience,' Leigh answered coldly. 'You seem to forget that you're slightly newer at this game than I am.' She stared straight into his eyes and felt, not for the first time, a giddy sensation of falling. She had noticed it the very first time they had met, and with every subsequent meeting that unsteadying feeling seemed to get more pronounced. She would have to get used to him if she was going to be living under the same roof.

'OK,' he said after a longish pause, 'I take your point.'

'You *what*?'

'Take your point,' he repeated in an aggravatingly measured voice. 'Now, if we could discuss schooling...' he continued, as though the two were linked in some way.

'What about schooling?'

'It'll be too far for you to take her to the school she's in now when you move to Hampstead.'

'I'll start looking at the situation soon.'

'Soon might not be soon enough.'

'Don't you think Amy will have had enough changes, without throwing a change of school in as well?'

'Some might say that it's better to do it all in one go so that there are no more nasty surprises in store.'

'Some might,' Leigh agreed, her voice implying that she wasn't to be counted in that number.

'There is an excellent independent school twenty minutes' drive away from my house.'

'I'll think about it,' Leigh muttered vaguely, pulling open the front door just in case he didn't get the message that it was time for him to leave.

'No need,' Nicholas said smoothly, stepping out into the darkness. He leant so that he was close to her and his breath was fanning her cheek. 'I've already sorted it out. Amy will start there after the Christmas holidays. All you really need to do is check out the business of school uniforms.'

'What? Why are you doing this? Why are you running our lives? When I came to you I didn't expect you to jump in and take over!'

'No, you most certainly didn't, did you?' he responded silkily. 'You simply expected me to hand over the necessary amount of guilt money and leave you in peace to get on with things. Well, lady, you misread the situation completely. We are not talking about donations to a good cause and we're not talking about any damn child. We're talking about *my* child, and I fully intend to get involved so that when *I* decide that the time is right to tell her who I am she will already have accepted my role in her life. Do you understand me or do I need to repeat what I have just said?'

Was it any wonder, she thought, that I dislike the man?

She had opened a door, not knowing what was behind it, and now it was too late to shut it back. Nicholas Kendall had taken over. It made no difference that he had offered her the best escape she could have hoped for; it made no difference that he had every right to sweep his daughter into his life.

Logic and reason compelled her to acknowledge everything he was doing on Amy's behalf, but his aggressive intrusion into their lives unsettled her. *He* unsettled her. When she was around him her entire body seemed to shift into another gear and she didn't like the feeling.

Leigh looked at her watch with mounting exasperation. Nicholas was due to collect her and take her to his house so that she could put her mind at ease that Amy wasn't going to be living in some terrible den of iniquity. What about me? she thought, not for the first time since this wonderful idea had been unveiled. *What about me?* She hated herself for being selfish, but she felt as though she had somehow been railroaded into a situation which she had neither invited nor wanted, and the worst of it was that she had no choice in the matter because the welfare of her niece came first, and quite rightly so.

She had begun stage two of the waiting game, and was pacing the floors of the sitting room when she heard his car pull up outside, then the slam of the car door and the sound of footsteps up the front path. She didn't give him time to use the buzzer. Instead, she flew to the front door, pulled it open and said tersely, 'You're late.'

He had taken the day off work and was wearing a thick cream pullover, greenish trousers and his Burberry, which he hadn't bothered to button up. Nor had he shaved. There was a hint of stubble on his chin. It gave him a rakish, piratical air of decadence, which seemed to her entirely appropriate, given his personality. Just the sort of man to enjoy looting and plundering and generally making himself unpopular.

'Eight minutes,' he said, looking at his watch.

Leigh didn't answer. She turned her back on him, flung on her coat as well as a trench coat—but black and of an infinitely cheaper variety than his—and gathered up her knapsack from the table in the hall.

'Have you told Amy anything yet?' he asked, once they were in his car and slowly heading down roads which didn't look in the least familiar to her.

'No.' The answer sounded so stark that she felt morally obliged to expand. 'She's all caught up in Nativity rehearsals at school. It just didn't seem the right time.' Naturally, she wanted Nicholas to go to the play. He impressed Amy, Leigh knew, and it was not just the abundance of gifts that he had thus far trailed in his wake. He impressed her the way he doubtless impressed most of the female sex, whatever their age. And perhaps, Leigh conceded, she was subconsciously trying to find another father figure. Little did she know.

'And when exactly is this "right time" going to come about?' he asked, and she could hear his temper just beneath the surface. He was allowing her to take the lead, even though the decisions had been made, *his* decisions, but his patience wasn't going to hold out for ever. Right now he was prepared to give her the benefit of the doubt because circumstances dictated it, but she was on probation. He somehow managed to make that patently clear.

'This isn't the easiest situation in the world, you know.'

'And you're not exactly helping matters either, are you?' He shot her a glance out of the corner of his eye and Leigh's lips tightened in self-defence.

When Amy was around they could just about manage to sustain their façade of politeness, but without her there they were like two adversaries, circling one another, ready to attack.

'Maybe,' he said, his voice hardening. 'I should take

Amy aside myself and tell her the truth, that she'll be coming to live in my house, that she'll be changing schools—'

'No!' Leigh looked at him with horror. 'It's taken her a long time to climb out of the shell she built around herself when Roy and Jenny died. I want to break it to her gently, a bit at a time.'

'Fine. Then I expect you to have started doing just that the next time I see you.'

'And if I don't? If *I* decide that Amy will be better off living without you on the scene?'

'You won't.'

'Because?'

'Because I say so.'

Leigh shot him a withering glance, but what else could she say? Her hands were tied and they both knew it.

'Have you handed in your notice as yet?' he asked, after a while.

'Not quite.'

'Does that mean no?'

'I shall do it some time this week.' Were there no areas of her life that hadn't been taken over by this man? Although she had to admit that handing in her notice would be something of a pleasure.

'And you can recommence your art course.'

'You remembered,' she said, surprised, and he glanced briefly in her direction.

'I have no idea how old you are, but you look barely out of your teens. I should imagine that your life has been immeasurably altered by what's happened. If you had any sense you would stop trying to fight me and start seeing this arrangement as an opportunity to return to something you loved.'

'I would rather have done it on my own,' she told him bluntly.

'But you can't,' he countered smoothly. 'I'm employing you to look after Amy and giving you the freedom to pursue your art during the day when she's at school. Surely that's the best of all possible worlds.'

Leigh didn't say anything. She looked at him surreptitiously, resenting his control over her life. 'Why are you offering to pay me for something I would do voluntarily?' she asked, and he shrugged.

'Do you want the truth?'

'Yes.'

'Because, despite what you so obviously think, I'm not in favour of taking advantage of people. I have no intention of compromising your pride. It must have taken a great deal to come to me in the first place.

'And what if you decide to sack me?'

'The situation won't arise.'

'Oh, let me guess. Because you say so, and we lesser mortals must simply trust in your greater wisdom.'

He laughed. It was the first time she had heard any real amusement in his voice, and the sound of his laughter sent disturbing little waves racing through her. For a fleeting instant she could see very clearly the charm, lying just below the surface, and this, like his unexpected laughter, was also disturbing.

She hadn't noticed the car slowing down and turning through a handsome pair of gates, more suited to announce entry to a country house instead of a Victorian house in the heart of London.

When Nicholas had told her that he lived in a three-storey house she had mentally struck off the penthouse idea and replaced it with a red brick affair stuck in the middle of other similar properties. She had been very far from the truth. The car glided between the gates and stopped in front of a magnificent house with a garden—and not just an apology for a garden, but a proper garden—with grass and fruit trees and a greenhouse at the side.

'I thought,' he said, looking at the expression on her face, 'that we'd have a quick look around. I'll show you where you and Amy will be. Then I've made an appointment for you to see the school. We can have lunch somewhere and you can ask me any questions you want to.'

Inside, the house was warm after the chill outside. It wasn't a mansion, but there was something indefinably tasteful and cosy about it. They were in a smallish hall, carpeted in deep red and with just the right amount of antique furniture to stop short of looking cluttered. Upstairs, there was the sound of a vacuum-cleaner, and Nicholas, following the direction of her eyes, said as he walked through one of the doors, 'Mrs MacBride. She comes in every day to do the cleaning and keep things ticking over.'

Leigh wasn't really listening. She was silently absorbing the house. The decor was impeccable. The furniture, the rugs strewn here and there, the paintings on the walls, all spoke of the elegant understatement that money could buy. There was nothing ostentatious anywhere.

He showed her around, not at great speed but not stopping anywhere to linger either, until they were on the third floor, where he showed her the rooms that she and Amy would be occupying—two bedrooms, with a small sitting room between them, and a bathroom, which was almost as big as the sitting room.

'It's completely self-contained,' he said. 'Occasionally it's been used for guests who stay overnight, but not very often. Most of the people I know live in Central London, and those who don't stay over at the country house.'

'The country house?'

'Didn't I mention it? My parents left it to me. It's in Warwickshire. Somewhat more sprawling than this.'

They went back downstairs, and Leigh turned to him and said in an embarrassed rush, 'Look, I feel I ought to mention this. I'm not altogether happy about…sharing a house with you.' He stared at her and she wished he wouldn't. It only succeeded in addling her still further. 'I know that you're rich and powerful and I expect that London is riddled with minions running around who would do anything for you, but I really don't know what kind of *person* you are.'

He relaxed with his hands in his pockets and his head slightly inclined, as though trying to read unspoken messages behind the words.

'I can't possibly tell you what sort of person I am. How the hell can I? In this sort of situation, you simply have to trust.'

She didn't look at him but her cheeks were flaming red. 'I also read, scouring through the newspapers, that you have something of a…reputation.'

'Oh, yes?'

She inhaled deeply and forced herself to meet his eyes.

Now, to her further humiliation, he began to smile. 'My intentions, I assure you, are perfectly above board.' He looked frighteningly sexy when he smiled, she thought with a shiver of awareness. 'I give you my word that you can rest safely tucked up in your bed at night, without fear that I'm going to burst through the door in search of sex.'

By now Leigh wished that the ground would open up and swallow her. Or, even better, open up and swallow *him*.

'I'm not implying...' Not implying what? Her mind came to a grinding halt.

'Look, to put it plainly, you're a child.'

'I most certainly am not!'

'No?' He raised his eyebrows, still amused. 'Perhaps that's the wrong way of putting it.'

'There's no *right* way of putting it,' Leigh said stiffly and with all the composure left at her command. 'I know exactly what you're saying,' She could feel the tiny pulse in her neck beating hard. She had a vision of herself—short hair, boyish build, flat chest, an androgynous, gamin figure, with all the wealth of her inexperience showing in her face.

'No, you absolutely do not know exactly what I'm saying.'

She didn't want to hear this. On the other hand, some masochistic instinct made her yearn to hear every unpleasant word.

'There's no need to elaborate,' she said, before he could launch into a sarcastic diatribe on her lack of feminine graces. 'We all have our types, and I'm very relieved, actually, that you've been honest with me.'

'Are you?'

'I most certainly am. Definitely.' She wished in passing that she had a long mane of hair which she could have tossed dismissively over one shoulder.

'Good.' He smiled and began to walk towards her. When he was next to her he paused, bent slightly and whispered, 'But what about me? How do I know that *I'm* safe?'

'Because,' she said, staring straight ahead of her, 'you're as little my type as I am yours.'

'And what *is* your type?'

'I happen to like caring, sensitive, artistic men.' She thought of Mick, her vanished ex-boyfriend, and conveniently chose to forget how much he had irritated her.

'Oh, what a relief. Now, shall we continue with the rest of the day?' He moved away and began to put on his coat, and she slowly turned around to look at him. All that masculine appeal, she thought, definitely not for me. She found that she was breathing a great deal easier now that there was some distance between them.

'Just one more question,' she said.

'Which is?'

'What about your lodger?'

'What *about* my lodger?' His voice remained exactly the same, but she had a swift, powerful feeling that something within him had stiffened at the mention of his lodger. Why did he have a lodger, anyway? Most peculiar.

'Where does he live?'

'It's not a *he*, it's a *she*.'

'Well, where does *she* live?'

'Is it relevant?'

'Who is she?' Leigh asked, made curious more by his lack of response on the subject than because she really cared one way or the other.

'A friend of the family,' Nicholas told her abruptly. 'And she lives in the converted basement.'

Leigh frowned and imagined a harmless old lady, a great-aunt of sorts. It would make sense if he was taking care of some ageing, distant relative who had nowhere else to live. It was also reassuring to know that there would be someone else in the house—another female.

'So, does she have meals with you?' she asked, more out of politeness than anything else. She pictured a cosy scene of Nicholas and his great-aunt, sharing dinner every so often. With this mysterious family friend, or relation, or whatever, in the background, she suddenly felt a great deal less daunted at the prospect of moving in.

'She has her own access to where she lives and comes and goes as she pleases. Now, if we could...' he consulted his watch then looked at her '...wrap up this subject and move on?'

'Of course.' She snapped out of her reverie. 'Where to now?'

'The school. While we're on that subject, do you drive?'

'I have my licence,' Leigh answered, 'but no car. For a while, after the accident, I drove Jen's, but we had to sell it to help pay off some of the debts.'

'How do you get Amy to school?' he asked, as he manoeuvred the car out of the drive.

'Walk.' She looked sideways at him and added cryptically, 'It's what those things called legs were made for, after all.'

'Well, the school we're about to see is too far from the house to make walking an option...'

'There must be a bus, in that case.'

'Perhaps. It's immaterial, anyway, because I shall be getting you a small, run-around car—'

'Don't be ridiculous!'

'I'm not.' He shot her a look, half frowning. 'And I hope that damned pride of yours isn't going to get in the way of common sense.'

'Pride? *Pride?* One minute I'm a gold-digger, and after whatever I can get my hands on. The next minute I'm too proud to accept anything from you! Could you make your mind up?'

He laughed under his breath. '*Touché,*' he remarked. 'However, a car would make life a lot easier for you.'

'I'm sure it would but—'

'No buts. I intend to get it. If you decide not to drive it then by all means feel free to leave it standing in the garage. You're quite welcome to spend forty minutes fighting your way to school on public transport.'

Which reduced her to silence, as he no doubt, she thought, knew that it would.

The school further proved the efficiency with which he got his own way. It was everything she could possibly want in a school for her niece. There was not a single flaw she could find, and she could tell from the satisfied smile on his face as they left that he knew exactly what she was thinking.

'So,' he said, over lunch, 'any questions?'

'You seem to have sorted everything out,' Leigh conceded, racking her brains to come up with some clever point he might have missed.

'Now, there's just the question of when you and Amy will be moving in.'

'After Christmas?'

'Why wait?'

'It seems the most convenient time. I mean, I wouldn't want to disrupt any plans you may have made.' Once again she had the unnerving sensation of being caught on a runaway train.

'I'll be the one to decide whether to disrupt my plans or not. As for the question of convenience, the sooner you move the better. I get the feeling that you may have one foot through the door, but the other foot is poised to take flight at the slightest opportunity.'

'I don't know what gives you that impression,' Leigh said, reddening.

'The fact that you seem unconvinced that you did the right thing in coming to me.'

Was she that transparent? Or was he just very astute when it came to reading other people's personalities? Either way, it was something she found vaguely disconcerting. She didn't want to be transparent. There was nothing mysterious in transparency.

Why do I want to be mysterious? she thought. What a ridiculous notion. She had never had any admiration for women who played coy games and cultivated the dubious habit of saying one thing and meaning another. She preferred the forthright approach. So why did it sting a little that Nicholas Kendall's impression was that she was an emotional and sexual simpleton, barely out of high school?

'What about the weekend?' he was saying, and she dragged her thoughts back to the matter in hand.

'*This* weekend?' She looked at him with openmouthed amazement, as though the suggestion had come totally out of the blue. 'Move? Into your house?'

'Correct on all three counts.'

'That's too soon. This is all happening way too fast. Amy barely knows you!'

'Which is something that can be rectified when she moves into my house.'

'Has it occurred to you that you might just succeed in frightening her off?'

'No, and I don't think it's occurred to you either.'

'It's just a little too...rushed,' Leigh persisted stubbornly.

'Why?'

'Because... Amy's school... The trip there and back...'

'Will take half an hour. If I recall, you were prepared to keep her there indefinitely, inconvenient or not.'

'That's not the point.'

'It's precisely the point.' He leaned towards her. 'You came to me, Leigh Walker. You waltzed into my life with a bomb in your hand. But my world has its rules.'

'So you keep saying, and I'm more than prepared to recognise that you're her father and you have a say in what she does, but until recently you haven't been a fixture in her life...'

'Which, as we both know only too well, had nothing to do with me!'

She ignored the bite in his voice and ploughed on. 'That's not the point. The point is that I know her better than you do and, while I'm ready enough to compromise, I won't be steamrollered into anything. I'll discuss it with Amy and let you know.' She wasn't looking at him. 'If I think that it's going to be too upsetting for her, the suddenness of it all, then you're just going to have to take my word for it and postpone it until she's become accustomed to the idea.'

'Fine,' he replied curtly. 'Just so long as this isn't a ploy to stall what has to be done.'

'Why should I want do to that?' Leigh looked at him with what she hoped was wide-eyed innocence.

'Because,' Nicholas snapped, 'it would simply be far more comfortable for you if my only contribution involved money.'

'Oh, we're back to that now, are we?'

He didn't bother to reply to that. He signalled for the bill, paid, without looking at the amount—a habit which

Leigh viewed with great disapproval—then said, as they sipped the remainder of their coffee. 'What about furniture?'

'I have a few sentimental things I'd like to bring with me, nothing very cumbersome, and, of course, there are all Amy's toys. The rest I'm quite happy to sell. What's left of it, anyway. Quite a bit had to be sold off during the course of the last few months to go towards expenses.'

'You should have come to me sooner. But let's not get into that.' He gave a short, mirthless laugh and leaned back in his chair so that he could cross his legs.

'No,' Leigh said awkwardly. What was it about his body, reclining in the chair like that, that brought to mind images of something untamed, darkly and unashamedly powerful? She found herself picturing those long, clever fingers, caressing, touching, exciting. She blinked rapidly, alarmed at that sudden meandering of her thoughts, and it occurred to her that at no point had there been any mention of a woman. Was he involved with anyone? Surely that might change with the addition of a young child?

'What are you thinking?'

She refocused her eyes on him. 'Why do you ask?'

'Because your face is very expressive. You're too young to have learnt the art of concealing your thoughts.'

'Please stop referring to me as *young*.' She looked at him, unexpectedly insulted by his description. 'And it just occurred to me that I don't know whether or not you're...involved with anyone.'

'No, you don't, do you? Why does it matter one way or the other?'

'Because,' Leigh said patiently, 'a woman might not

take kindly to discovering that you have a seven-year-old daughter.'

'If a problem of that nature arises,' he drawled, 'you'll be the first to know.'

Which didn't say anything much but now that her mind had turned to the possibility it seemed intent on dwelling on images of women, women to whom he might be attracted. He had made it abundantly clear that *young* wasn't his type, and she imagined that he would be attracted to mature, voluptuous women with big breasts and full, pouting lips. Blonde, bouffant hair everywhere, she supposed. High heels and long, red nails.

'And for that matter,' he was saying. 'I don't want you to feel that your social life is in any way restricted by living under my roof. No more than it was restricted before.'

Did she have a social life? Of sorts, she supposed. She had kept in touch with her friends from art college, and occasionally they went to the movies or out for a cheap meal, but with Amy that had become difficult, and now cheap meals out in the evening had been replaced by quick lunches and, of course, there was no boyfriend.

'Thank you,' she said politely.

'Male friends can come and go, but clearly within limits.'

What was that supposed to mean? 'I don't entertain an entourage of men,' she informed him coolly.

'No.' He looked at her lazily. 'I wouldn't have thought so, but I felt I might as well make the point.'

The point being, she thought later, that women like me don't attract men in droves. The point being that I am, in fact, one of the genderless.

She told herself that she was relieved at that because sexual attraction was the very last thing she wanted.

CHAPTER FIVE

THERE was no yell of joy down the telephone line when Leigh told Nicholas that she had decided that they would be moving in on the weekend. His voice was clipped and she imagined him sitting in front of his desk, impatiently waiting for her to say what she had to say and clear off the line so that he could get back to the tiring business of running his empire.

Over the past couple of days she had done rather more delving into his background. She had gone to the library during her lunch-hours and buried her head in business magazines, flicking through countless articles. She had even managed to locate a centre spread on the rise and rise of Nicholas Kendall, which had been written only a few months previously when he had launched a successful take-over of an ailing automotive components firm.

It seemed that in addition to the sprawling network of businesses, inherited from his father, his heart lay in the buying of sick firms, which he then proceeded to turn into viable concerns to be sold later at great profit. A few were listed in the article and there appeared to be no common link between them, which seemed to be where his genius lay. He could turn anything around.

There was a picture of him, standing amidst the employees of one such firm, and they all appeared to be smiling, which led her to think that they had either been drugged into acquiescence for the photo or else they didn't know the first thing about Nicholas Kendall at all.

She searched very carefully for any revelations about his private life, any indication of women lurking in the background, but the *Financial Times* and other such publications were clearly uninterested in Nicholas Kendall, the private man.

'I can't talk at the moment,' she heard him saying, which instantly made her hackles rise. 'Meet me at the club in forty minutes.'

'I'm at work,' Leigh informed him. Did he think that she was lazing about at home, doing nothing in particular?

'Leave it.'

And he replaced the receiver so that the argument forming on her lips was cut off before it could even begin.

Throughout the entire trip by Underground and foot to his club she could feel her temper mounting.

If this sort of summary approach was any indication of what it would be like to work for him then she would have to tactfully inform him that it wasn't going to work out. Did he simply imagine that she was at his beck and call, whatever the time of day or night?

She arrived at the club ten minutes late, and was shown immediately to the sitting room, where he was waiting for her with his briefcase open on the small, round table in front of him, talking into his cellphone. He waved her to sit down and continued his conversation, without looking at her.

He had removed his jacket, which was slung over the back of the spare chair, and his shirtsleeves were rolled to the elbows.

Leigh sat back in her chair, crossed her legs and scrutinised him from under her lashes. He was purported to be something of a financial wizard in the City. His pronouncements were treated with respect and the merest hint that he might be buying a company was often enough to send its shares soaring.

When he had finished talking on the telephone he clicked it off, stuck it in his briefcase and afforded her a long look.

'Right.'

'There was really no need for you to drag yourself away from your desk to meet me here,' Leigh said, fairly ungraciously. 'I really only phoned you to say that we will be able to move in on the weekend after all.'

'Have a cup of coffee.'

There was a tray on the table with various silver jugs and a plate of oddly shaped, home-made biscuits. He poured her a cup and handed it to her.

'I'm out of the country until Friday and it's better if we discuss arrangements face to face. I take it that Amy was not too alarmed at the prospect of moving house?'

Actually, there had been no scene at all. She had accepted the proposal with the unquestioning, placid acceptance that children sometimes showed in the face of what most adults would consider monumental upheavals.

When? had been her first question, and Leigh had thought, *When?* What about how come? Or, since when do we know that man well enough to move in with him? Or even, I don't want to leave my home.

'I managed to persuade her that your kind offer had come at a very good moment, what with the bank about to take the house, and that it might be a good idea to move in sooner rather than later. Of course, she's a little bit nervous about the whole thing. I mean, you can understand that. She barely knows you.'

'I like him,' Amy had said when Leigh had asked her

what she thought of Nicholas Kendall. 'I think he's kind.' It had flashed through her head that 'kind' was hardly the word to describe someone basically mean, ruthless, domineering, overbearing and arrogant.

'Are you sure that you're not describing your own reactions to the prospect of moving in with me?'

Leigh reddened and sought temporary refuge in her cup of coffee. 'I'm not in the least nervous about the move, as a matter of fact. However—' she eyed him unwaveringly '—since you're going to be employing me I think we should be quite clear on what the job entails.'

His eyebrows shot up in surprise at that. 'Precisely what you're doing at the moment, I should think.'

'That's fine because I really objected to being summoned away from my job today.'

'If you're expecting an apology for that you're wasting your time.' He sipped his coffee and looked at her over the rim of his cup. 'For a start, I take it you've already handed in your notice...'

'Yes, but—'

'Secondly, you hate the place...'

'Hate is a bit strong—'

'Thirdly, you spend quite a bit of time correctly pointing out to me that Amy must come first so you can hardly object when I ask to meet you for the expressed purpose of discussing her.' His mobile phone buzzed, and he pressed a button to switch it off. 'Now, arrangements. I'll send someone along to do all the packing. You'll simply have to point out what's to be taken and what's to be left. There's nothing terribly big to be transported so a sizeable van should be sufficient.'

'There's really no need for you to trouble yourself,' Leigh said quickly. 'It'll be more tiring to have to direct

someone to what can and can't be packed. I'll make sure
that it's all done by Saturday morning.'

'You hate this, don't you?' he asked, after they had
agreed on times and Leigh had started wondering
whether she wasn't beginning to consume too much of
his valuable working time.

'What?' She deliberately misunderstood the question,
but from the expression on his face she had not managed
to fool him.

'The way events have taken a turn in your life.'

'I'm cautious, that's all.'

'That's understandable.'

'I mean, fatherhood has been thrust onto you but you
don't know the first thing about what it's like, having a
child live under your roof. Are you still going to be
enthusiastic after two months? Six? A year? You won't
be able to return her to a shop, you know. You might
well be her natural father but, let's face it, you probably
know your paper boy better than you know your own
daughter.'

His eyes had turned wintry. He slowly deposited his
cup on the table and leant towards her with his elbows
on his knees.

'Let's get something very straight here, Miss Walker.
You seem to consider it perfectly acceptable to set yourself up as judge and jury on me and my lifestyle. Sure,
you have your doubts and I can understand that, but I
am frankly sick to death of your sweeping assumptions
and moralising. If Amy senses in any way whatsoever
that your heart isn't in this move it won't be long before
she begins to feel uncertain, and *I will not have that
happening*.'

Leigh's body had become rigid and she could hardly
breathe, although this was far less to do with anger than

with the mortifying knowledge that there was an element of truth in what he was saying.

'You may dislike me, but you'll be civil. Do you understand?' he hissed.

'There's no need to treat me like a child!' She found that she was whispering as well, although there was no one else in the room with them. This just wasn't the sort of place for making a scene.

'If you act like a child you'll be treated as one.'

Leigh stared at him at a loss for words, and finally he shook his head impatiently.

'There's that look again.'

'What look?'

'That huge-eyed, innocent look.'

'That gets on your nerves... I do apologise...' She could feel tears stinging the backs of her eyes. Was she childish? Yes. Yes, she supposed she was. She had always been looked after, cosseted by her parents and by a sister who had been old enough to have seen her as a baby to be indulged and protected. When their parents had died Jenny had soothed her, looked after her, put her needs first, taken over the role of parent. And moving on to art college had hardly hardened her.

Now here she was, dealing with responsibilities that she had never had before—dealing with a man whose only experience of women was of the sophisticated variety. She had been forced to grow up and she had, but underneath there was still the young girl, trying hard to be strong. She had been strong when Jenny and Roy had died, strong for Amy's sake. She had been strong when her relationship with Mick had crumbled around her. She had developed the necessary veneer to take her through the thin times. But she wasn't strong with this man.

'Don't damn well apologise. It wasn't meant to be an

insult.' He paused and very nearly smiled. 'You're an utter contradiction, do you know that?' He looked at his watch and closed his briefcase. 'Is it all settled about the weekend, then?'

Leigh stood up and nodded, tugging down her dreary black skirt and attempting to look practical and businesslike.

'I'll be over to help some time during the morning, and—' He stood up, put on his jacket and said, before she could interrupt, 'Don't tell me that there's no need to trouble myself.' He straightened, looked at her so thoroughly that her skin began to prickle and graced her with another of those slow, amused smiles which she found so disorienting.

'There's no need to trouble yourself,' she said, with a smile of her own, then she ducked and began to precede him to the door.

What, she thought later, had *that* been all about? One minute she had been angry and insulted by his scathing directness and then, quite suddenly, something had altered, although for the life of her she couldn't put her finger on it. All she knew was that by the time they had parted company outside the club her heart had been pounding like a drum in her chest.

Was it because she was so inexperienced when it came to men that she simply found it difficult to handle those lightning shifts in his moods?

She stuffed the niggling questions to the back of her mind and concentrated on the ordeal of relieving drawers and cupboards of what progressively was turning into a treasure trove of unplumbed trivia, all of which needed to be sorted out bit by laborious bit.

It was just as well that she had now left her job. Her boss, with aggravating and long-winded petulance, had finally allowed her to leave, without giving her full month's notice, and she needed the time to pack.

She accomplished during the day a large amount when Amy was at school, not wanting her to come across anything that might open floodgates to memories of her parents. But in the evenings Amy insisted on helping, which was more of a hindrance than otherwise. The little things which had to be wrapped were wrapped with such infinite care that the process took ten times longer than if Leigh had done it herself. And then there were the inevitable discoveries of outdated toys, which were greeted like old friends and promptly added to the ever-increasing pile of things to be taken to Nicholas's house.

By Saturday morning there was five times more to transfer than Leigh had intended. The van turned up promptly, and forty minutes later, true to his word, so did Nicholas, dressed in what he doubtless considered old clothes for the job at hand.

'I'm sorry,' she said, as soon as he had entered the house, 'there was more than I expected. Bits and pieces. I hope you don't mind.' Her voice was very adult and very polite because she had decided since last setting eyes on him that she was *not* going to act like a pre-pubescent child. She would not allow him to reduce her to self-conscious uncertainty.

She had made a concentrated effort to put the man into perspective, and the fact was that he was Amy's father, a virtual stranger who had entered her life through a back door of sorts. His presence in her life was one of necessity and not choice. They were two utterly different human beings who had been brought together by outside circumstances.

In the normal course of events, they would never have met and, even if they had, they would never have spared one another a second look. So, she had told herself, what he said, what he did, could not possibly have any real impact on her. It made sense when she thought about it logically.

Amy, who was sitting on the sofa with a book on her lap, looked up and said with stunning self-confidence, 'I told Leigh that you wouldn't.'

Nicholas smiled and there, in that slow, charming, warm smile, was the reason why he had managed to climb so quickly into Amy's affections and why her description of him had been of someone kind and thoughtful.

'It's a big house,' he said, walking over to where she was and squatting down on the floor by her so that he was on her level. He glanced at the cover of the book, then looked at his daughter. 'Big enough to hold any number of things you might want to bring over.'

'How big?' Amy asked with interest, and Nicholas described his house to her, but not in estate agent jargon—in funny language a child could understand. He told her that it had been standing there, just waiting for a child like her to come along, and Leigh felt a lump in her throat at this obvious corny, tear-jerking remark. Well, he certainly knew how to lay it on, she thought, and her heart clenched with apprehension as she took in Amy's pleased face.

If you hurt her, she thought, you'll have me to answer to.

'Shall we go?' she asked in a voice that was more glacial than she had intended, and they looked at her in unison. It was an eerie feeling, seeing the striking similarity at such close quarters. Just looking at them there, they seemed to *belong*.

'I take it that only one trip will be necessary?'

Nicholas asked, straightening. The charm had dropped from his face, and his eyes were as cool as her voice had been a minute ago.

'Oh, yes.' Leigh forced a smile on her face for Amy's sake and was relieved when she got a smile back in return. 'I'll just check the rooms before we go. Make sure that we haven't forgotten anything. Not that it's the end of the world if we have.'

She left them where they were. She had been afraid that when the final hour came, and the front door of the house was closed behind them for good, Amy would break down, but when she returned to the sitting room half an hour later Nicholas had managed to engage Amy's attention. He had brought a tiny computer toy with him, small enough to fit in the palm of his hand, and he was explaining the mechanics of it to her.

They left the house, with Amy deeply absorbed in whatever it was that he had given her, and Leigh shot him a look of gratitude.

'Good idea,' she said to him, once they were in his car and driving away. She half nodded in the direction of the back seat. 'I was a bit worried...'

'Mmm. Yes. Quite. A difficult time potentially.'

They were speaking in code, although Amy's attention was very far removed from their conversation.

'And you?' he asked conversationally, sparing her a fleeting sideways glance. 'OK?'

She was so surprised by this rudimentary show of interest that she replied without the normal wariness she tended to adopt when in his presence.

'I guess.' She sighed and shrugged. 'Moving on.'

'Yes. Always hard.' They had stopped at some traffic lights and he turned to look at her. Their eyes tangled for longer than she intended, and she was the first to look away.

From the back seat the computer toy was emanating strange, high noises, and Leigh covered her momentary confusion by swivelling around in her seat and asking Amy to explain how it worked.

'You press this button,' she said obligingly, holding out the toy so that Leigh could pretend to inspect it, even though her eyes could barely focus on what was in front of her. In this position her face was only inches away from Nicholas's shoulder, and she was shocked to realise how intensely his proximity was affecting her.

'And it does what?'

'Move that figure...there... You've got to get him to attack those little blobs... See there! Like that...'

'And then what happens?'

'And then you get points at the end of the game.'

'And then what?' Leigh asked, squinting at the hand-held toy.

'And then,' Nicholas said, with a throaty chuckle, 'you become nauseatingly addicted to repeating the exercise all over again and beating your previous score.'

Leigh shifted back into her seat and looked at his amused profile. 'It doesn't seem to be a very constructive way of spending one's time,' she told him, perplexed.

'You're an artist. Your definition of a constructive way of spending one's time is to create something.' He shot her a glance, then redirected his attention to the road ahead. 'You grew up with paper and colours and paint.'

'Papers and colours and paint are still in existence, believe it or not.' The beeping noises were still coming from the back seat, accompanied by exclamations of delight, closely followed by moans of disgust.

'But computers have now been added to the equation.'

'I don't know a thing about computers.'

'You must have used one in your job,' Nicholas said, glancing in his rear-view mirror to make sure that the van was behind them.

'Electric typewriter, thank heavens. I don't trust those things.'

'You think that they'll explode if you press the wrong button?' he teased. 'Come to life and stage a take-over?'

'Well, we've all seen the movies,' she said.

From behind Amy asked. 'What movies?'

'Computers, taking over the world,' Leigh said, laughing. She relaxed, feeling young and carefree for the first time in months.

'That's ridiculous,' Amy said, laughing as well. 'They can't *do* that. You just never use them!'

'You tell her,' Nicholas encouraged.

Leigh could feel an immense sense of well-being steal over her and through her, filling her up, and she found herself idly wishing that this car drive could continue for ever.

It was only as they began to slow down and turned right into a driveway that she pulled herself back together. And it was only as they were getting the things unloaded from the van and taken into the house that she realised how thoroughly Nicholas had managed to remove all the tension from her shoulders. Tension which had been with her from the day her sister had died. Tension which had been with her, it seemed, from way back before that.

She looked at him as he strode up the stairs ahead of her, with Amy following closely, and wondered how on earth he had succeeded in doing that. How had he? She didn't even like the man!

He was directing things into rooms while Amy opened

doors, peered inside and asked questions, thoroughly un-inhibited.

'You can help me with my toys,' she said to him, and they stood in the middle of a pile of boxes while Amy surveyed her quarters.

'I'll leave you to it,' Leigh said to them, and promptly did. She headed for the other bedroom and carefully began to unpack her own belongings—clothes, some books, a few ornaments, her art equipment. She had enrolled at the college to start at the beginning of the next term, and just the feel of her brushes and the caked surface of the toolbox which she used to store her paints was like the touch of a familiar friend.

Her back was to the door when she heard a voice behind her. 'There's a room on the floor below that you can use as a studio if you like.'

She swung round to find Nicholas, lounging against the doorframe, and she immediately wondered how long he had been standing there, watching her. Then she laughed the notion away.

Did she imagine that because he was friendly for half an hour in a car that he suddenly found her attractive? With her short hair and her coltish body and her freckles? Not to mention her unspeakably faded attire, which she had donned because moving was a fairly messy business.

'That's very kind,' she said awkwardly from her position on the floor, where she was kneeling to inspect her art box. She slammed down the lid and stood up hurriedly, brushing her clothes with one hand.

'Have you enrolled in your...college?'

'To start next term.' They looked at each other and Leigh broke into hurried speech. 'The hours are perfect. I shall be able to drop Amy off at school and collect her in the afternoons, and I can always paint after she's gone to bed. Much better than when I worked, as a matter of fact.' She heard herself babbling on with something approaching dismay. 'It was always a mad dash to get to her school on time.' Her voice petered out, and to her consternation he appeared in no hurry to break the silence, which left her gazing awkwardly at him while her hands fidgeted nervously together.

'Has Amy finished unpacking?' she asked eventually. 'I should go and check on her or else she'll get swamped by her things and forget that the object of the exercise is to put them away.' She looked down at her feet, shoeless because she had removed her trainers, and then at her hands, which she forced to her sides because twining them together was so indicative of her nervousness and there was no sane reason why she should be feeling nervous.

'She's engrossed in her unpacking,' Nicholas said. 'Leave her to it.'

'Right.'

A further silence fell. Leigh cleared her throat meaningfully and hazarded a full look at him.

'I'll be down in a minute.'

'Your portfolio.' He nodded to her bed and she followed his gaze. 'May I have a look?'

Absolutely not was her first, panicky thought, but hard on the heels of this instinctive reaction was the acknowledgement that she was quite prepared to show her work to all and sundry so why on earth not him? She nodded and watched as he unclasped it and looked through the contents, holding them out and inspecting them. Eventually he said, without looking at her, 'Artists are very sensitive about criticism, aren't they?'

'Very,' she agreed, blushing, 'so please feel free to lie.'

'I expected something more abstract.'

'I'm a rather boring painter,' Leigh told him, cutting short any temptation on his part to waffle on about the merits of abstract art. 'There's so much beauty around— why distort it?'

'Why, indeed.' He returned her canvasses to the portfolio, snapped it shut and stood back with his hands in his pockets. Separated by the width of the room, she was still profoundly aware of him—of his overpowering masculinity.

'I like them,' he told her, and she nodded and muttered her thanks. 'They're very vibrant, very emotional.' He paused and then said musingly, 'Do you ever dress like the woman I would have described as being behind those paintings?'

'What do you mean?' It was all she could do to get the words out with some semblance of nonchalance.

'Bright colours.' He shrugged and continued to look at her. 'A little on the wild side, I suppose.'

'Me? No, I don't think so.' She didn't care for the turn in the conversation at all.

'Shame. It would be interesting…' He moved towards her and she felt a flare of panic, excitement and apprehension run through her like an electric current.

It was a feeling she had never experienced before. It made every nerve in her body tingle.

He stopped in front of her and looked at her upturned face. 'To see whether your art is saying something that you're afraid to say yourself.' He didn't lay a finger on her, but still her breath caught in her throat and her body was aching as though he had touched her. She wasn't wearing a bra and she could feel her nipples push against her shirt, throbbing.

Her mind toyed with images of his lips against hers, his hands pushing beneath the shirt to caress her breasts.

'Lunch will be in half an hour,' he said, and she blinked rapidly and returned to the present, shocked at her reaction to him—stunned at the treachery of her body, which had responded with such blatant arousal to a situation which had not even existed. 'Edie—Mrs MacBride—is doing something light.'

His voice was so normal that she wondered how on earth she could have leapfrogged into a scenario that had no grounding in reality.

She drew back from him and folded her arms, which at least stopped them from trembling.

'Something light's fine.'

'I don't like salads,' Amy said from the doorway, and they both turned to look at her.

'I'm sure Mrs MacBride has seen fit to do something a little more than a couple of lettuce leaves, Ames,' Leigh said, with a deep feeling of relief that her niece had appeared at precisely the right time.

'You'll have to fill her in on your likes and dislikes,' Nicholas said. Was it her imagination or had he drawn away slightly as well?

'Oh, I don't think so!' Leigh laughed. 'Or else we'll be having chicken nuggets and pizzas every night of the week.'

'What's wrong with that?' Amy grinned, and in the middle of this Nicholas headed off, pausing on the way out to inform his daughter that there was probably more nutrition in the packaging than there was in a plateful of chicken nuggets.

PLAY...

"ROLL A DOUBLE!"

GET 2 BOOKS
AND A
FABULOUS MYSTERY BONUS GIFT

ABSOLUTELY FREE!

SEE INSIDE...

(U-H-P-11/98) 106 HDL CJRA

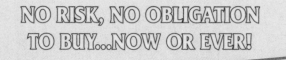

GUARANTEED

PLAY "ROLL A DOUBLE" AND YOU GET FREE GIFTS! HERE'S HOW TO PLAY:

1. Peel off label from front cover. Place it in space provided at right. With a coin, carefully scratch off the silver dice. Then check the claim chart to see what we have for you – TWO FREE BOOKS and a mystery gift – ALL YOURS! ALL FREE!

2. Send back this card and you'll receive brand-new Harlequin Presents® novels. These books have a cover price of $3.75 each, but they are yours to keep absolutely free.

3. There's no catch. You're under no obligation to buy anything. We charge nothing – ZERO – for your first shipment. And you don't have to make any minimum number of purchases – not even one!

4. The fact is, thousands of readers enjoy receiving books by mail from the Harlequin Reader Service®. They like the convenience of home delivery...they like getting the best new novels BEFORE they're available in stores...and they love our discount prices!

5. We hope that after receiving your free books you'll want to remain a subscriber. But the choice is yours – to continue or cancel any time at all! So why not take us up on our invitation, with no risk of any kind. You'll be glad you did!

The Harlequin Reader Service®—Here's how it works:

If offer card is missing write to: Harlequin Reader Service, 3010 Walden Ave., P.O. Box 1867, Buffalo NY 14240-1867

BUSINESS REPLY MAIL
FIRST-CLASS MAIL   PERMIT NO. 717   BUFFALO, NY

POSTAGE WILL BE PAID BY ADDRESSEE

HARLEQUIN READER SERVICE
3010 WALDEN AVE
PO BOX 1867
BUFFALO NY 14240-9952

NO POSTAGE
NECESSARY
IF MAILED
IN THE
UNITED STATES

'Not,' he added, 'that I'm entirely sure what a nugget is.'

As soon as he had left the room Leigh could feel her breathing return to normal. She continued with her unpacking. She forfeited the shower until after lunch, chatting with Amy in a voice that was way too bright to be normal while her head frantically tried to grapple with her feelings.

Had Mick *ever* made her feel that way? Produced that helpless, yearning sensation inside her? No. Theirs had been a relationship that they had somehow drifted into, but now, when she thought back to him, all she could remember with any clarity was his childish irresponsibility. When they had both been carefree students she had found that charming—a symbol of freedom, of someone who refused to conform. Later, when responsibilities had begun to pile on top of her, she had seen it as weakness.

When she had needed a shoulder to cry on he had not been there because he simply did not possess the strength to give her. It was as if life within the art college had been life within a vacuum. Circumstances had forced her out of the vacuum, and she had had to take a deep breath and struggle out of the cocoon into reality.

Mick, she had soon realised, would never undergo that struggle and nor had he wanted to. And wasn't it just as well in the end? She couldn't picture him in this sort of environment at all.

She glanced around her at the accumulation of wealth—all the rewards of hard work and long hours and the powerful, clever mind of someone who never shied away from the responsibilities that life had had to offer.

Wasn't that why Nicholas Kendall had assumed the welfare of this unexpected daughter with such gusto?

She and Amy headed down to the kitchen. She had managed to put those puzzling reactions to him to the back of her mind. She had a job to do, and do it she would without distraction, least of all distraction from a man who, essentially, belonged to a different world.

He was standing by the dresser with a cup in his hand, and seated at the kitchen table, in the relaxed pose of someone who belonged there, was the most beautiful woman Leigh had ever seen in her life.

She was easily into her thirties, possibly late thirties, but her skin was alabaster smooth and her blonde hair was swept back into something very clever at her nape.

She had obviously been deep in conversation with Nicholas because as she turned to the door to look at Leigh her mouth was still slightly open, as though a sentence, half formed, was waiting to come out. It was a very photogenic pose, almost unnatural, but, then, Leigh thought beauty often appeared that way. Contrived, artificial, splendidly untouchable.

'This is Fiona,' Nicholas said, pushing himself away from the dresser to pour Amy a glass of orange juice. 'My lodger.'

Leigh gave her a perfunctory smile. His *lodger*? Surely not. His lodger, according to her imagination, was old and comfortable and grandmotherly.

'So *you're* Leigh Walker,' Fiona stood up. She had a long, elegant body, the sort that complemented whatever happened to be thrown over it—designer outfit or dustbin bag. Either would look spectacular. 'And *you*...' She smiled at Amy who stared back at her with the intense, penetrating stare that only children could use without embarrassment. 'You must be little Amy.'

'I'm sorry.' Leigh looked at Nicholas with some confusion, 'I didn't know that you had company.'

'Oh, never mind me!' Fiona said gaily. 'Just pretend I'm not here, darling.'

'Fiona's just dropped in for a quick cup of coffee,' Nicholas said to Leigh, and there was an undercurrent of amusement in his eyes as he took in her awkwardness.

She knew why. No wonder he considered her young and infantile if he based his comparisons on Fiona, who was theatrically draining the remnants of her cup and attempting to win Amy over with another incandescent smile.

'Oh, darling, she's *gorgeous*.' She walked gracefully over to Nicholas and placed her hand on his arm. 'You're an absolute *doll*, aren't you?' she said to Amy, who had finished her juice and was carefully putting the empty glass on the kitchen counter.

'Thank you,' Amy said politely, looking at Fiona with the quizzical expression of someone viewing a madman's antics. Leigh stifled a laugh.

'You ought to see her when she's in her stunning floral ensemble,' Leigh said, keeping a straight face with difficulty and trying to imagine her niece's horrified reaction should she ever produce any such outfit for her to wear. 'All bows and frills and matching hat with black patent shoes.'

'Yuck!' Amy burst out laughing, and Nicholas grinned at Fiona, who seemed piqued that her compliment had not found its target. '*No one* wears that sort of stuff at my age!'

'Kids these days.' Leigh shook her head with exaggerated regret, and received a scathing look of dislike from Fiona. 'Leggings and jumpers and black Doc Martin boots.'

'A bit like you, my dear?' Fiona said, with a cool little smile.

'I'm afraid so,' Leigh replied flippantly, biting down hard on the hostility that was rising in her like bile.

'Lunch is ready in the dining room,' Nicholas said, moving towards the kitchen door and collecting Amy *en route*. He glanced over his shoulder at Fiona. 'How long are you going to be in the country?' he asked, almost as an afterthought.

'Only a couple of days.' She looked sideways at Leigh. 'But after that who knows?'

Leigh began to follow in the safer direction of the dining room, but before she could make it to the kitchen door Fiona stopped her. Nicholas and Amy had already vanished.

'I do hope you don't get any ideas into your head about Nicholas,' she said softly, still smiling.

'What are you talking about?'

'I'm talking about you living here under his roof. Nick can be a very charming man. From one woman to another, I wouldn't want to see you get hurt.'

Leigh felt the blood rush to her face and she had to steady herself against the doorframe.

'There's no possibility of that happening,' she muttered.

'I'm so glad to hear that because, sweet as you no doubt are, Nicholas has never had much time for little girls. He prefers women.' Like me, her voice said. She gave another quick, cold smile and then she walked off, and Leigh made her way slowly and thoughtfully into the dining room.

CHAPTER SIX

LEIGH didn't know what she should expect by way of Fiona, popping up with more of her venomous warnings. She had visions of having to creep through the house and peer around corners but, as it turned out, over the next few weeks she only happened to see her in passing on a few occasions.

She had tried to prise information subtly out of Nicholas, but all she knew for sure was that Fiona worked as a buyer for a fashion house and so spent a great deal of time out of the country.

But what, she wondered, was she doing in *his* house? She surely must be able to afford somewhere of her own.

Not that it matters one way or another, she told herself over and over again. So what if she and Nicholas were having some kind of affair? The few times she had spotted Fiona had certainly been at night. She'd been dressed to the nines and having a drink with Nicholas, and Leigh could only assume that these were preludes to dinner or the theatre or some other, more exotic destination.

It preyed on her mind.

She restlessly tossed around images of him with the elegant blonde, making elegant conversation followed by elegant love. Every time her mind travelled down that route she told herself, very firmly, that Nicholas Kendall could do as he pleased—she really couldn't give a damn.

She had other things to worry about. She had to make sure that Amy adapted to her new surroundings. She spent a great deal of time helping Amy with her homework, playing with her before bed in the small sitting room on the top floor and making her bedroom as warm and inviting as possible.

Nicholas had bought her a poster of Winnie the Pooh, for which Amy thanked him profusely, and, having ascertained that it would be all right to stick a poster on the wall, promptly replaced it with one of a pop group, much to Nicholas's amusement.

Everything appeared to have settled into a pleasant routine.

Nicholas came home in the evenings, generally just before Amy was ready to go to bed, and he would always spend some time with her, listening to her read a book or chatting. Occasionally he would read her a story, but Amy told him frankly that his stories were a bit too childish. She preferred the gory to the sugary.

At those times Leigh would tactfully vanish after a few pleasantries, and there was usually no need to clap eyes on him again for the night as she ate an early supper with her niece.

So she saw relatively little of Nicholas. A few times he had chatted with her after Amy had gone to bed about her school and how she was doing generally. She had managed to train herself not to react to his presence at times like these.

But curiosity nagged at the back of her mind over his relationship with Fiona. *Was* she his personal life? Or did he have a personal life somewhere else? He went out a great deal at night, but where she had no idea.

She had been doing some painting in the studio, which she now used regularly, practising her art before college began the following January, when, on the spur of the moment, she decided to hunt out Nicholas. She knew he was around. Somewhere. He had tucked Amy in for the night as usual and had informed her on his way out that he would be in if she wanted to have an evening out with her friends.

The weather had turned bitterly cold in the past few days, from gold autumn to the grey white of winter. Even inside the house, with the radiators pumping out heat, it was still cool enough for Leigh to have flung on a jumper over her T-shirt earlier on when she had gone down to the studio to paint.

If he's in his bedroom, she told herself, it'll wait.

He wasn't. She checked the kitchen first, which was in darkness, then the sitting room, which was lit but empty, and had already decided that he was in his bedroom when she noticed a thin strip of light under the study door and from inside the deep timbre of his voice.

She stood, poised for instant flight, outside the door, listening to ascertain whether there was someone in the room with him. At times like this, she thought guiltily, a glass would come in handy.

After a couple of minutes she knocked, and only realised how little she actually wanted to be there when she found herself in the study. There was no going back now, of course.

He had been speaking into a dictating machine, which he now clicked off, swivelling around in his chair so that he could look at her. The computer terminal, which was on the desk in front of him, was turned on, and the screen showed what appeared to be financial data. How long had he been in here, working? It was already after nine-thirty. Did the man never stop?

'Yes?' he said, more in surprise than irritation.

Leigh stood by the door with her hands behind her back, and tried to remember what she had come to say.

'I'm sorry to disturb you.'

He didn't say anything. He pressed his thumbs against his eyes, stood, switched off the computer terminal and said, without looking at her, 'Don't be. I've had enough of these figures anyway.'

'I thought we might have a quick chat about Amy.'

'Is there a problem?' he asked sharply, turning to face her, and she shook her head.

'No. Just a couple of points.'

'Let's go into the sitting room. More comfortable there.'

Leigh wasn't quite sure whether she wanted comfort, but she followed him and accepted a gin and tonic when he poured one for himself.

'Now,' he said, sitting on the chair opposite her, 'what's the matter?' He took a long, slow mouthful of his drink and stretched out his legs in front of him, crossing them at the ankles.

'Just to let you know that I've spoken to her about changing schools.'

'When?'

'This evening,' Leigh admitted.

'And? Her reaction?'

'She's a little bit put out at the prospect of having to move, and make new friends.'

'Did you explain why it was necessary?'

'I told her that the school she's going to now is a little too far. She seemed fine. She's become a little scared of changes in her life, what with one thing and another.'

'She seems to have settled down all right here, though.'

'Yes. She has.'

'No complaints that I don't know about?'

'No.'

'Would you tell me?'

She hesitated. 'I suppose so, yes.'

'Good. Let's not forget that I'm her father. I don't expect you to keep anything from me.' He finished his drink and regarded her steadily, with the glass still in his hand.

'I haven't forgotten,' she retorted quickly.

'Which brings me to something I've been meaning to talk to you about.'

'Yes?' Her stomach gave a little flip. Why did that have such an ominous ring to it?

'We need to decide when would be the best time to tell her who I am.'

'Not yet!' Her reaction was automatic. She could not envisage any such possibility in the near future, even though she knew that he wouldn't be prepared to continue with his farcical role of family friend for ever.

'When?' he asked. His voice was steely. He was asking a question to which he wanted an answer.

'Well, it's not the sort of thing I can pencil in for a date,' Leigh prevaricated. 'I'm just not sure whether she's ready or not for that kind of revelation. As far as she's concerned, Roy was her father.'

'But,' Nicholas said smoothly, 'he *wasn't* her father. *I'm* her father and I don't intend to remain in this role for the rest of my days.'

'I know that!' she told him, restlessly finishing her drink. She allowed him to take her glass to be refilled, even though she could feel the alcohol fizzing through her, making her even more jumpy and on edge.

He strolled across to the bar, poured them both another drink and handed her the glass.

'No,' he said, 'I don't think you do. I think you're quite prepared to allow this situation to carry on indefinitely, by which time it'll be doubly difficult to tell her.'

'No, it won't.'

'She'll wonder why nothing was mentioned sooner. Also, from my point of view, I'm obliged to take an interested back seat when it comes to making decisions about her future.' He crossed his legs and looked at her steadily. 'Then there's the fact that as a family friend—' his mouth twisted cynically when he said this '—I can neither guide nor reprimand her. I'm on the outside, looking in, and I don't care for it.'

'I get your point, but you'll just have to bear with us for a bit longer.' Two gin and tonics was definitely not a good idea. Her head was beginning to feel a little heavy and she had to concentrate on every word he was saying.

'I would like your definition of ''a bit longer''.'

'A few months, maybe,' Leigh told him vaguely.

'Not good enough.'

'What are you saying? I can't be any more definite than that.'

'Then I'll fill in the gaps on your behalf, shall I?'' He rested one hand along the arm of the chair and drummed on it steadily and softly with his finger. Leigh watched, mesmerised, until she forced herself to tear her attention away from the rhythmic movement back to his face. 'The year is practically finished. Amy starts her new school at the beginning of next year. I intend to give her a while to settle in then I shall break the news to her, with or without your co-operation.'

Leigh could feel colour rise to her face. 'In other words, although you pay me to take care of your daughter, I have no final say in anything. Is that it? I could be anybody. My duties are simply to make sure that Amy is fed, looked after, clothed, dropped at school and collected.'

'Don't be ridiculous. That's not what I'm saying at all.' He shook his head, as though clearing it of something irritating. 'You provide moral backbone for her, and I am very grateful for that. However, you do not have sole charge over her.'

'I've had sole charge for the past eighteen months!'

'The situation has changed.' He sighed. 'You're being obstinate,' he said. 'Why? Are you afraid of what will happen to you when Amy is told who I am?'

Leigh shot him a bewildered look from under her lashes. No, she had not been afraid of that at all. In fact, the thought had never crossed her mind. It began to cross it now.

What *would* be her position once his fatherhood was established? Right now, his hands were more or less tied. He was obliged to endure her presence because he knew that Amy depended on her, but he had already made deep inroads into his daughter's affections. Amy responded to him.

On weekends they would disappear for hours on a stretch, and Leigh would come across them in the office, playing on his computer or sitting in front of a chess board while he patiently explained the rules of the game. They seemed to click without any effort at all.

She had no idea if this was because of their natural bond or whether their minds just worked along the same lines. Both were logical people who enjoyed things that adhered to a clean, clear, mathematical guideline.

Roy, she thought, had been wonderful with her. He'd taken her for walks and played ball in the garden, but she'd been five and a half then. Time had passed, and there was a great deal of difference between a five-year-old and a seven-year-old.

The time was fast approaching when Nicholas would

become another important fixture in Amy's life, and when she learned that he was her father what would her, Leigh's, role be?

A time scale had never been mentioned and Leigh had never thought to ask. She had been too focused on the present, on just making sure that each day passed smoothly. But what if her role was purely transitional? What then?

'What *will* happen?' she asked now.

'You're young. You have your life stretching out in front of you.' He shrugged. 'I don't expect you'll want to live under this roof for the rest of your life.'

'I hadn't thought,' Leigh mumbled uncomfortably. Was she supposed to suggest a deadline as to when she would be ready to move out? And what when she did? She didn't want to lose touch with her niece.

'I'm not suggesting that you pack your bags,' Nicholas told her, watching her closely.

Not yet, she thought miserably.

Maybe he had an agenda, though. Fiona was discreetly tucked away at the moment, an unobtrusive third party. Were they both waiting until the time was right? Her gut went into spasms at the thought of Fiona taking over the nurture of her niece. She would make a lousy mother. Couldn't he see that? What, she thought, had she condemned Amy to?

She stood up and felt a little wobbly on her feet.

'I think it's time I headed off to bed now,' she muttered under her breath. She felt ill. Whether it was from the drink or from the implications now buzzing in her head she wasn't sure. She leaned for a moment against the back of the chair to steady herself, and when she glanced at him she saw that he was looking at her with an expression of consternation on his face.

'I'll help you up,' he said, standing and moving across to her.

'I'm fine!'

'No, you're not. You're white, like a sheet.'

She felt his hand on her arm and she made a desultory effort to brush it away. She didn't want him near her. She felt giddy and frantically worried that Amy was now doomed to see her beloved mother replaced by an ogre like Fiona.

She had visions of house rules that included no loud laughter and no talking during meals and a boarding school tucked away somewhere in the remote country-side of Devon—somewhere so far away that it would be very difficult for her to ever see her niece again. Of a finishing school in Switzerland, where Amy would be disciplined into a miniature replica of Fiona.

'Take your hands off me!' she snapped at Nicholas, struggling to forcibly remove his hand from her arm.

'What the hell is the matter with you?'

'I just want you to leave me alone!'

'Oh, for God's sake!' He bent slightly, and before she knew what he was going to do he scooped her up as easily as if she weighed nothing.

Leigh wriggled in embarrassment and horror. His hands against her seemed to burn through her jumper and travel through her T-shirt until they collided with flesh. Since he showed no inclination to deposit her on the ground, she gave up the unequal battle and allowed herself to be taken up the stairs into her bedroom and placed on her bed, from where she eyed him nervously as he loomed above her.

She didn't dare relax, even though her body felt weak and boneless, so she adopted a half-sitting position against the pillows and continued to stare at him, wishing he would leave.

He didn't. He sat on the bed next to her, and she pushed herself up a bit further against the headboard.

'Two gin and tonics might have been a little optimistic,' he drawled. 'Why didn't you tell me that you weren't accustomed to alcohol?'

The shame of it all. Her cheeks flamed.

'I thought it might be nice to try a change from my usual diet of orange squash and lemonade,' Leigh retorted tightly, and Nicholas laughed under his breath.

'That would explain it, then,' he told her, shaking his head slightly and still grinning. She could have hit him. 'Are you going to be fit to climb out of your clothes and get into your pyjamas?'

'Are you suggesting that you lend a hand?' she answered back, stung by his amusement. 'All part and parcel of your role as my employer?'

'You're a stubborn minx, do you know that?'

'I am nothing of the sort. You're just an overbearing, demanding, unbearable…' Her voice spluttered into silence, and they looked at one another in the shadowy half-light of the bedroom. His face seemed more angled in this light. She could not quite make out the colour of his eyes. They appeared darker, more brooding. The curve of his mouth, half smiling at what she had just said, was frighteningly sensual.

She felt her pulses quicken and every nerve in her body seemed to have awakened and become acutely sensitised to his proximity.

He leaned slightly and propped himself up, with his hands on either side of her.

'You can be so flattering when you put your mind to it,' he murmured.

Leigh opened her mouth and discovered that she couldn't say anything. Her vocal chords had seized up. What if Amy were to burst in on this little scene? she thought. But Amy's bedroom was separated from hers by the sitting room in the middle and, anyway, there was no chance of her waking up. She could sleep through an earthquake. Besides, what scene? Leigh thought.

'I just resent—' she began. He dipped his head, and as her eyes closed his mouth touched hers. Strong, cool lips pressed hers open and found the inviting warmth of her tongue. He moved one hand to cup her face, and she gave a spontaneous little groan as his kiss deepened, and his questing mouth became hungrier, pushing harder so that she was pressed against the headboard.

All thought and reason had taken flight. She curled her fingers into his hair, arching her body until she felt as though she were being absorbed by the urgency of his mouth.

When his hand left her face and dropped to her waist her breathing quickened.

Then she felt his fingers spread underneath her jumper, underneath the T-shirt, flat against her stomach, travelling upwards until they were caressing the small, firm swell of her breast. She moaned, a gentle sound, and wriggled slightly as his thumb found her aching nipple and teased it into a responsive peak.

Her entire body was melting, or at least that was what it felt like. Dissolving. She could feel the moistness between her thighs and she ached for his hand to explore there, to touch her, to open her up with his fingers.

But he didn't. He sat back and looked at her with shock, and it was only then that her mind began to function once again. She thought with horror at what had very nearly happened. They stared in silence at one another, then he said roughly, 'I have no idea what happened there.' He pushed himself off the bed, and his withdrawal from her was like having a bucket of ice cold water flung over her.

All trace of dizziness had vanished. 'No,' she managed to say in a whisper.

'I must have taken leave of my senses.' He raked his fingers through his hair and prowled around the room, before standing in front of her once again. 'I can only apologise—' he began, and she cut him short before he could continue.

'Don't!' She didn't want to hear what an awful mistake he had made. She didn't want him to say what he was so obviously thinking—that she was the last woman in the world he could ever be attracted to, but he had touched her in a moment of madness and she had responded. 'It was a mistake.' Her voice was clear but unsteady. 'It won't happen again, and I don't want a post-mortem on the incident.' 'Incident' seemed to reduce it to what it was—a momentary lapse that could be papered over and then safely ignored.

She had yanked down her jumper, but her T-shirt underneath was still rucked up above her breasts. Her voice and her head were saying one thing, but she was humiliatingly aware that her nipples, still hard and throbbing, were craving the feel of his fingers, the wetness of his mouth.

She was sorely tempted to ask him, coldly, whether he saw sex as part of her nanny duties, but that would have been wildly hypocritical because she knew that she had wanted him—probably a lot more than he had wanted her. The knowledge only added to her mortification.

'I think it's best if you leave,' she told him quietly.

He looked at her in silence for such a long time that she began to feel uncomfortable. What was he thinking? No, she didn't want to know.

When he finally did leave the room she remained where she was for a long time, staring at the closed door and desperately trying not to pin down her thoughts because she was terrified of what she would find.

Eventually, she slipped off the bed and lost herself in a long, hot bath. But a long, hot bath could not wash away what had taken root in her mind.

Over the next week, when she saw him in the evenings in the company of Amy, her mouth politely responded to his questions but underneath she could feel the stirring of her body at the memory of what had happened.

He showed no acknowledgement in his face that anything had taken place between them, and for that she was grateful.

She immersed herself in sufficient things during the day to keep her mind on harmless things. She almost forgot that Fiona existed until, on the Friday night, as she was pouring herself a glass of milk in the kitchen, she heard footsteps behind her. She swung around, already composing her features into a bland, smiling, unrevealing mask.

She had expected Nicholas so Fiona was almost a relief. The other woman had obviously just returned from work. She was wearing an emerald green suit, totally unsuitable, Leigh thought, for icy pavements and howling winds but, then, she supposed that fashion buyers did not frequent the Underground, and only actually trod on pavements so that they could hail a taxi.

Leigh swallowed her milk with extraordinary speed, and set down the empty glass on the kitchen counter.

'We haven't crossed paths for quite a while,' Fiona said, depositing her bag on the table and folding her arms.

'I don't think that Nicholas is about.' Why bother with polite chit-chat?

'No, he's out with clients.'

So, Leigh thought with a jealous pang, she knows his whereabouts. I'm only the nanny. Of course he won't give me a typed itinerary of his comings and goings.

'I was just on my way out,' she said hedging towards the door. 'I only came down for a glass of milk.'

'Milk. How virtuous. Accompanied by a few cookies, no doubt?' There was no pretence of amicability in Fiona's voice, and the hard, smooth face was antagonistic.

'Yes, that's right, accompanied by a few cookies.' Leigh sighed wearily, not wanting to embark on a vitriolic clash of words.

'Is that the image you're taking such pains to convey? The milk and cookie girl who never wears make-up and dresses down in jeans?'

'I'm not trying to convey any image,' Leigh told her tightly. 'Now, if you'd excuse me.'

'It won't work, you know. I've already told you that and I'm going to repeat it.'

'I have no idea what you're talking about.'

'Of course you have so you can wipe that innocent look off your face. There are just the two of us in the kitchen now so no need to pretend. Nicholas has told me about the plans the two of you have made for Christmas.'

'He has?' Leigh stopped and frowned. Plans? What plans? This was news to her.

'Yes, he has,' Fiona spat out. 'The three of you up in

the country house. Very cosy. Log fires and Christmas tree, and Santa Claus, clambering down the chimney.'

Leigh looked at the other woman, astonished and then angrier by the second at arrangements which appeared to have been made without her consent. She wasn't going to show any of this, however. Oh, no, she would wait until Nicholas came home and then she would ask him what the hell he thought he was playing at. Why bother to go through the motions of consulting her on anything when he had his own private agenda and planned to do precisely as he pleased?

'Don't think that I'm going to sit on the sidelines while you try and wheedle your way into his bed,' Fiona said, her fingernails digging into her arms.

'I have nothing to say to you about any of this,' Leigh returned swiftly. 'What you and Nicholas have... going...is none of my business, and that's the way I intend it to stay.' Over my dead body, she thought. Once and for all, I'm going to find out what's going on. She knew that a deep, confusing, biting jealousy was spurring her on, but she didn't care.

She walked out of the kitchen, ignoring the glittering rage in Fiona's eyes, and resolutely stationed herself in the sitting room to wait for Nicholas's arrival.

She switched on the lamp by the chair and after an hour fell asleep, to be awakened, much later, by the overhead light being turned on and the sight of Nicholas standing over her, his jacket slung over one shoulder and one hand thrust into the pocket of his trousers.

'What time is it?' She surfaced groggily, rubbing her eyes. When he told her that it was after eleven she sat up straighter as her mind focused and she remembered what she was doing down here.

'Get to bed,' he said roughly, as she put her hands to

her hair and tried to fashion it out of its rumpled state into something a little more orderly. He turned away, but she stopped him before he could leave.

'I want to have a word with you,' she said coldly, and he half turned to look at her.

'What about? Surely it can wait until tomorrow morning.'

'No, I don't think it can.'

'Well, what is it?' He remained leaning against the doorframe, looking at her, and she wondered what he was seeing. A young, unsophisticated, gauche ex-art student, she supposed, dressed in very unprepossessing jeans with an oversize white shirt slung over them, curled up on a chair. She though of Fiona in her emerald green suit and felt the same surge of the anger that had assailed her earlier in the kitchen.

'I had a visit from your...lodger. She tells me that you've apparently made plans for us for Christmas. Without even bothering to consult me! I'm sick of this, Nicholas!'

'You waited up to tell me that?' He made it sound as though she had waited up to tell him that she had chipped her fingernail.

'Yes! I happen to think it important that I'm at least *consulted* before you go...arranging things behind my back! And then telling the whole world about it before you choose to inform me!'

'They weren't *plans*,' Nicholas grated. 'I happened to tell Fiona that I was thinking along those lines. I had every intention of filling you in when I next saw you.'

'Filling me in? Don't you think that Amy and I might have made alternate arrangements?'

'Have you?'

'I *was* thinking about spending Christmas Day with

Carol and David, our old next-door neighbours,' Leigh said. 'We spent Christmas there last year and it was very pleasant.'

'Well, think again. This year you're spending it with me.'

'Thanks very much for your willingness to discuss the subject,' she snapped, feeling thoroughly weary and exploited.

'Look.' He walked towards her and sat on the edge of the low, square table in front of her. 'What's the problem here? I would like to spend Christmas with my daughter.'

'There's no problem,' Leigh told him coolly. 'I would just appreciate it if you allowed me to have some say in the matter, instead of being informed of things via your lodger, or girlfriend, or whatever she is.'

She gave him a glassy-eyed stare. 'What *is* she, exactly, by the way?'

'I don't see the relevance.'

'Well, I do. Are you planning on forming some little family unit once I'm out of the way?'

'Don't be absurd.' His face had hardened. He didn't want her prying into his private life, but she was damned if she was going to maintain a tactful silence just to accommodate him.

'I am *not* being absurd, and I think I deserve an answer. Amy is my niece, and I'm not asking this out of curiosity but because her welfare has to be taken into account.' And Fiona, she thought viciously, would make about as good a mother substitute as a black widow spider.

'If it makes any difference whatsoever, Fiona is the daughter of my parents' friends. She's been living in Paris for the past eight years, and when she got a transfer to London it was suggested by her father that I put her up until she found somewhere else to live.'

'And how long ago was that?'

'Does it matter?' He sighed impatiently. 'Seven months.'

'Seven months, and still nowhere has turned up? How convenient for both of you. I don't know why you've stuck her down in the basement, though,' she continued, masochistically relishing every word and knowing that she would regret her impulse later. 'Surely there's enough space in the house for her?'

'I think you and your over-fertile imagination should get yourselves to bed.'

She'd thought she might have antagonised him with her insinuations, but she hadn't. If anything, he sounded amused, which made her madder because his amusement reduced her remarks to the level of a childish outburst. He could laugh at what she said, she thought, because he had no intention of paying a scrap of attention to a word she was saying, and he certainly had even less intention of divulging the details of his private life.

Why should he? He would hardly admit that the wedding ring was lined up when he clearly knew how she felt on the matter.

'Me and my over-fertile imagination,' she said with freezing politeness, 'would like answers to our questions.'

He stood up and half yawned.

'Go to bed, Leigh.' He paused and then said in a lazy, speculative voice, 'before I'm tempted to carry you there.'

That was sufficient. She walked quickly out of the

sitting room, fuming, feeling his eyes on her as she walked along the corridor.

Heaven only knew what plans he had for himself and Fiona and Amy, but she would go to hell and back rather than let them materialise.

CHAPTER SEVEN

ARRANGEMENTS for Christmas had now been formalised. The three of them would travel up to Nicholas's country house on Christmas Eve and would return to London on the day after Boxing Day.

Leigh, who could not enthusiastically imagine any plan that included herself and Nicholas cooped up at close quarters for any period of time, spent several days trying to work out how she could back out, but in the end she was sabotaged by Amy.

She was hovering in her niece's bedroom, clearing up books and toys, while Nicholas sat on the bed and chatted about the Nativity play—now over and done with in under forty minutes after weeks of frantic rehearsal—when she heard him say casually, 'So, where would you like to spend Christmas, Amy?'

Amy was looking at her father, beaming, still swept away at her fifty-second role of an elf in the play.

'Last year we went across to Sophie's mum and dad,' she said eventually.

'And wasn't it lovely, Ames?' Leigh said brightly, shoving books into the bookcase and glaring at Nicholas's back.

'But that was last year,' Nicholas told her. 'This year's going to be a little different. There are three of us now, and I wouldn't dream of celebrating Christmas on my own. Santa might bypass me completely unless I can persuade a certain seven-year-old girl to keep me company.'

'I'm sure,' Leigh interjected sarcastically from behind, 'that he wouldn't dream of doing any such thing, providing you've been a good little boy all year long.'

Nicholas ignored her input.

'I'm not sure I believe in Father Christmas,' Amy told him confidentially, 'I mean, how can he fly around the world in the space of just one night? And he *is* rather large to fit down chimneys, isn't he?'

Nicholas turned and looked at Leigh dubiously. 'I'm sure Leigh has the answer to your questions,' he said, grinning at her.

'Magic,' Leigh said vaguely.

'*Not!*' Amy grinned broadly. 'But, of course, he *might* be real,' she continued, hedging her bets and thinking of Christmas presents.

'I thought that we three might have a little holiday in the country,' Nicholas said, dragging the conversation back to the point in hand. 'I have a wonderful place in Warwickshire, surrounded by fields. There are even a couple of horses. They're a bit old, I admit, but not too old for a ride.'

And that had been that.

'Out and out bribery,' Leigh said later when they were in the kitchen, discussing the technicalities of driving up to Warwickshire with a boot full of presents.

Nicholas, who was sprawled in a chair, sipping his cup of coffee, raised one eyebrow in a question.

'Bribery? What on earth are you talking about? I merely told Amy that there were a couple of horses around.'

'You knew how she would react. How many seven-year-old children can resist the temptation of riding a horse?'

'Did you ride horses when you were seven?'

'No, but the temptation wasn't there.'

He shrugged. 'Well, I suppose, now that you mention it, it was something of an argument-clincher.' He stretched out his legs onto the chair in front and Leigh paused to look distastefully at him.

'That,' she said pointedly, ruffled because she felt that she had been railroaded into something she hadn't wanted and ashamed at her own selfishness, 'is unhygienic.'

He gave her a look that seemed to say it was his house, after all, then he appeared to think better of it and removed his feet from the chair.

'Not much time to work out turkeys and Christmas trees,' he said. 'In fact, just about a week.'

'You mean you haven't got an instant solution?' Leigh smiled sweetly at him. 'I would have thought that would have all been part of the master plan.'

'I'll give the Daleys a call tonight—get Marge to come in just before we arrive to air out the bedrooms.' He cradled the cup in his hands and stared at the dresser thoughtfully. 'She can buy all the food we'll need while we're there, and if Jo mounts a tree in the drawing room we can decorate it as soon as we arrive.'

Leigh, looking at him as he spoke aloud, felt something stir inside her. At times like these, when they weren't at each other's throats, she was overwhelmed by something very nearly like contentment. A certain peace. She had spent the past year and a half running at full speed, battling her way through problems and trying not to drown under the burden of financial worry. Now, listening as Nicholas took over, she felt utterly and blissfully relaxed.

It wouldn't last, of course. In a minute the questions would spring into her head again, but for the moment she drank her coffee, perched on a bar stool by the kitchen counter, and regarded him without suspicion.

'What did you do last Christmas?' she asked idly.

'Last Christmas,' he said, with an element of surprise in his voice, 'I was in the middle of a take-over, and I worked. Solidly.'

'Sounds fun.'

He looked at her cryptically from under his lashes. 'My, you *are* getting sarcastic in your old age, aren't you?'

Leigh went faintly pink. 'What about your parents?'

'Cruising in the Caribbean. Work sounded infinitely less exhausting.'

'And where are they this year?'

'At home in the South of France, with their vast assortment of friends.'

'You could always go there,' she suggested half-heartedly, and he looked at her, amused.

'And bypass the opportunity to get under your skin for days on end? Besides, I haven't spent Christmas in the company of a child for...for as long as I can remember...' He rose and stretched. 'Enough of this maudlin reminiscing. I have a mountain of work to do before we leave and now is as good a time as any to start doing it.'

Leigh felt a swift stab of disappointment at the thought of being left in the kitchen on her own. It was warm and cosy in here, with the wind blowing in a blustery fashion outside and rattling the window panes. She had never seriously envisaged what it would be like to have a family. Jenny had always been the one who had hankered after hearth and home, but now it occurred to her that there was something to be said for domesticity.

Her mind sprang ahead to when she would no longer

be wanted in this house—when Nicholas had established himself as Amy's father and her supporting role was over. When the curtain call came and it was time to leave. She tried to imagine the freedom of being able to do exactly as she pleased and found that she couldn't.

'Wake up.' He was standing right next to her, breathing into her ear, and she jumped.

'I thought you were going to do some work,' she said irritably. Her daydreaming had broken her fragile mood of tranquillity.

'I am, and it'll go so much quicker if I have someone to transcribe while I dictate.'

'In that case, I'm sure it won't be too difficult to get hold of one of your secretaries. They're probably poised by their telephones, just waiting for such a call to arms.' She slid off her kitchen stool, taking care to avoid coming into contact with him, and began to wash the few items of crockery in the sink.

'Half an hour,' he said, propping himself against the kitchen counter and watching her. 'A bit of typing. It would be a help.'

'I loathe typing,' Leigh told him, turning off the tap and removing her gloves. She faced him with her arms folded. 'Why do you think I hated working in an office?'

'But I'm sure you're very proficient at it.' He produced one of those blisteringly charming smiles of his. 'It'll save an awful lot of time, you know. We'll be able to get off to a much earlier start on Christmas Eve. Miss all that traffic. Get there in good time to decorate the tree. So much better than arriving in the dark, with Amy barely able to keep her eyes open in the back seat.'

'Oh,' Leigh said slowly, 'I get it. If I don't sit and play secretary it'll be all my fault if Christmas Eve turns into a disaster.'

'Well,' Nicholas shrugged his shoulders, not responding to her remark, 'up to you. I can't force you to do it. And I certainly don't want to be accused of taking advantage of your role of nanny here.'

Leigh looked at him with exasperation. 'OK!' she snapped. 'Your talent for bribery amazes me. What next?' she demanded, following him out of the kitchen towards the office at the end of the house. 'If I don't cook the Christmas lunch shall I be single-handedly responsible for all poor weather fronts, moving in from the Arctic and settling over your country estate?'

She could hear him whistle under his breath, pleased, she thought, with having got his own way. As usual.

'There, now,' he said soothingly, settling her into a leather chair by the desk and switching on the computer. 'Half an hour at the most. Stop me if you don't understand something or if I'm going too fast for you.'

He drew another chair close to hers, opened his briefcase and extracted a mound of paperwork.

'This is ridiculous,' Leigh muttered, staring at the screen which stared back at her, waiting for her input. Pressurised by her sister, she had done a six-month secretarial course after leaving school, but to sit in one spot, typing in other people's words, was a form of torture for her. Her job in an office had only slightly been alleviated by telephone calls to customers and paperwork, neither of which she found thrilling but both of which were preferable to typing. 'There's no way that this can possibly be listed as one of my duties, and I won't be helping you out again.'

'You can start with this letter,' he said, handing over a sheet of paper with his strong, black writing on it. 'I'll need three copies. You can use the fax machine for copying.'

Leigh glowered and started typing, while next to her Nicholas scribbled and amended and occasionally made a phone call, talking in curt monosyllables.

To her surprise, they worked quickly and efficiently together, although, as she had expected, the half-hour deadline had been wildly optimistic.

When he began dictating, prowling around the room restlessly as though movement enhanced his ability to think, she stopped typing, waited until he had finished his sentence and then said in her best secretarial voice, 'Some of this is grammatically incorrect.'

'Good girl! Then you can sort it out.' He grinned at her, and she refused to succumb to the humour.

'It's also after eleven. I thought you told me that we would be here for half an hour at the most.'

'Slight miscalculation.'

'I feel sorry for any poor woman who has the misfortune of working for you.'

'They love it, if you really want to know. I may get on your nerves some of the time but...' He moved swiftly to where she was sitting, leant over and said softly, 'I'm an absolute poppet to work for.'

Leigh bit back the inclination to laugh loudly at that and gave him a jaundiced look. 'And I'm from planet Mars,' she said.

'I doubt they're as attractive as you on Mars,' Nicholas told her, straightening, and for a split second there was something in his voice, some deep undertone, that made her skin begin to tingle.

Now that she thought about it, it was very intimate in this little office. It was a small room, with dark furnishings and fully stocked bookshelves. Nicholas used a single spotlight on the desk. Apart from that bright beam, illuminating the computer and an area of desk around it, the lighting in the room was subdued.

'Well...' She stood up and stretched, suddenly nervous and eager to be out. 'It's not too difficult, being more attractive than a small green alien with antennae. Anyway, we've been here...' she looked at her watch '...a little over two hours, and I think it's time I headed off to bed.'

She began to move towards the door and he said, without looking at her, 'Why don't we have a nightcap? Unwind a bit after all this.' He glanced across at her and the combination of the shadowy light and her sudden awareness of him made her lick her lips apprehensively. As she stood there, hesitating, debating what she could say to his suggestion that wouldn't sound puerile, he drawled, 'You don't seem terribly keen at the prospect of having a drink with me.'

'I'm just a little tired, that's all.'

'Tired or nervous?'

'Tired,' she said firmly, 'but I guess I could have a quick drink with you.' Coerced again, she thought. Made to feel, somehow, that declining his civilised offer would be a show of immaturity. Or maybe she was reading a little too much into the offer.

This time no gin and tonics, though, she decided. When he asked her what she would like she asked for a glass of white wine. After he had returned from the kitchen with it she settled down into the chair and sipped her drink, tucking her legs underneath her.

They spent a few minutes discussing this and that and nothing in particular, then he said in a musing voice, 'You're good at it, you know.'

'At what?'

'The secretarial bit. Transcribing. You're a quick

thinker. I've had hell with temps who have found it impossible to reorganise into lucid English what I've written down for them to type.'

'They probably describe it as having hell with bosses who write down in a disorganised manner what they're expect to type.'

He laughed appreciatively, and she felt that warmth run through her again. 'I don't suppose you would consider doing the occasional bit of secretarial work for me in the evenings. I would increase your salary, naturally.'

'Out of the question, I'm too exhausted by the end of the day to make this a habit. You only succeeded in talking me into it in the first place by using Amy as leverage.' She had another sip of wine and half closed her eyes.

'You're too young to be exhausted in the evenings. You should be out, going to clubs and parties and burning the candles at both ends.'

'I shall wait until I'm older to do that,' Leigh said, too tired to take offence at what he had said. 'In the meantime, I'll just give in to my exhaustion.'

He didn't say anything for a while and when she looked at him he was twirling his glass in his hands. 'I haven't noticed much social activity going on in the house,' he said finally, 'I don't want you to feel in any way restricted by the fact that it's not your place.'

'OK.'

'I mean, no men on the scene.' He swallowed a mouthful of wine and then reverted to playing with the glass, staring at the white liquid swirling around. 'Surely you must have recovered from your break-up with this character you were going out with.'

'That's absolutely none of your business.' More to the point, it was her cue to leave and get back to the sanctuary of her bedroom, but she couldn't be bothered. She would finish her drink and leave, she decided, in her own time. She wouldn't allow what she did to be dictated by her reactions to what he said to her.

'Have you recovered? Sometimes it helps to talk about these things.'

Leigh opened her eyes completely and gave him a long, hard, cynical look. 'And you're proposing to be my listening ear, is that it?'

'Something like that.'

'Thanks but, no, thanks.' She placed her glass carefully on the table next to her and rose to her feet. 'Before I fall asleep down here I think I'll head upstairs.'

He got up as well and moved to stand in front of her so that she was obliged to look up at him with an expression of puzzled politeness. What now? she wondered. His face, while not exactly annoyed, was slightly flushed.

'Why do you back off the minute I mention your sex life?'

'I don't back off,' Leigh told him, startled by his overreaction to her lack of response. 'I just prefer to keep my private life to myself.'

'I suppose it must have been difficult...with Amy...'

'I suppose, like I said, that it's none of your business.'

'Are you still carrying a torch for this man?'

Carrying a torch for Mick? The idea of it was almost enough to make her burst out laughing, but she had a feeling that reaction would not be appreciated.

Perhaps he really felt as though he could somehow help. Maybe he thought that she had some kind of sexual hang-up, and he felt sorry for her. Poor, immature Leigh Walker, too naïve to know how to deal with the opposite sex. If the women in his life were along the lines of

Fiona, she could see how he would have arrived at that conclusion.

Sophisticated, hard-headed women could protect themselves but women like her, she supposed, were the sort of miserable wretches who were too inexperienced in love to play the game. He probably thought that Mick had broken her heart and then walked out just when she'd needed him most.

'What if I were?' she asked with mild curiosity. 'What if I went to bed at night and was tormented by longing for my ex-boyfriend? Would you be able to produce a cure from up your sleeve?'

'I'd tell you that you'd be a damn fool to carry a torch for someone who walked away from you.'

'Well, on that note of wisdom, I think I'll bid you goodnight.' She waited for him to step aside. When he showed no inclination to do so she folded her arms, expelled a long, weary sigh and said, 'No, I am not carrying a torch for Mick, or for anyone else for that matter. I see my friends occasionally during the day. We meet for lunch or for coffee at Covent Garden. I guess I'm a boring little soul who shuns the night life. Satisfied?'

'There's no need to jump down my throat simply because I offer you a bit of advice,' he grated.

'Just stop thinking that you can get involved in my life! You're Amy's father, and we've been brought together by an odd twist of fate, but that's the end of it!'

'You live under my roof, and you're related to the daughter I never knew I had. Wouldn't it be a little strange if I was totally uninvolved with you?'

'Strange but welcome.' She tapped her fingers against her arms, and was about to produce a yawn—if only to show him how uninterested she was in anything he had to say about her personal life—when he pulled her arms down to her sides and pinned them there.

'And you can stop looking so damned bored and blasé!'

The suddenness of his action took her breath away. She stared at him in open-mouthed confusion.

'What right have you got to tell me how I should *look*?'

'No right at all,' he muttered. He cupped her face suddenly between his hands and a flare of panic ignited in her. She didn't want this. Last time she had been under the influence of two strong gin and tonics. This time there was no excuse, not even a limp one, and she didn't want this. She wanted him to leave her alone, to get out of her way so that she could go upstairs to the warm safety of her bed. She didn't want him touching her; she didn't need this frightening, gut-wrenching rush of adrenaline.

His mouth crushed hers with an urgency that stifled the protest in her throat. Her mind continued to warn her, to steer her away. Her lips, though, softened to meet his. The words of anger and outrage at what he was doing became a soft moan of pleasure.

She fought and struggled until he was compelled to release her arms. Her hands, which should have pushed him away, coiled at the back of his neck, urging him against her. Every muscle in her body told her that this was what she wanted, what she needed, what she had spent the past few days craving. The desire was so strong and so elemental that she felt as though she had been carrying it around with her all her life.

She could feel him pushing her back, still kissing her as he propelled her towards the rug in front of the fireplace.

It was a thick, Persian affair, very soft and luxurious. They sank onto the floor, and when she surfaced to breathe he caressed her neck with his mouth, wetly tracking down the pale column of her throat.

In the silence of the room their breathing seemed magnified, imbued with an urgency and hunger that she had never associated with making love. He was unbuttoning her shirt, spreading it open. She could feel the quick rise and fall of her breasts and she arched her back, fumbling behind her to unclasp her bra.

It was total madness, but driving need had replaced reason. She just wanted him.

As he pushed up the bra, now loosely lying over her breasts, she let out a whimper and curled her fingers into his hair. She guided him to one pink, taut nipple and shuddered as his mouth circled it, sucking it in, nibbling and teasing it with his tongue.

He was holding her hands apart, and she groaned as his exploring mouth caressed both breasts, licking and suckling on each nipple until she felt as though she would explode.

As soon as he released her hands she began to unbutton his shirt, trembling and eager to feel the firmness of his chest. He yanked the shirt out of the waistband of his trousers, sitting up so that he could remove it altogether, and she took the opportunity to look at him.

He was perfectly and powerfully built. The line of his body was so well defined that he would have been beautiful to sketch. There was an animal grace about him, and she continued to watch, mesmerised, as he removed his clothes, uninhibited by his nudity.

Then he undressed her until she was left in only her lacy underwear.

At the back of her mind, as he eased his body alongside hers, Leigh knew that something was happening, something that went beyond the simple act of making love, but what it was she lacked the concentration to explore. It was a question that hovered tantalisingly in the dim recesses of her brain, visible yet too opaque to be defined.

Not that she was capable of defining anything. Her body had come alive, and the stirring of sensations she'd never known existed thrilled and frightened her.

She turned on her side and wrapped one leg over his, and he kissed her lingeringly and lazily, caressing her breast as he did so. The frantic hunger had been refined into something less rushed and all the more erotic for that. It was as though time had slowed down, as if they were moving in a dream.

He licked her lips and she squirmed as his thumb and forefinger played with her hardened nipple. Pressed lightly against him, she could feel the stiffness of his arousal. She reached down to take it in one hand, luxuriating in his groans of pleasure as she moved her hand rhythmically up and down.

His hand circled her waist, stroking it, then he pushed her flat, and she could feel that craving mounting inside her again, like hot lava rising to overspill, as he trailed his mouth along her flat, firm stomach.

She parted her legs, and she could almost feel herself holding her breath in expectation of his caress.

Her hands rested lightly on his head. She feverishly opened her eyes and looked down as he moved lower, only closing them when his tongue began to explore her, plunging deep, lightly teasing, flicking and setting her alight.

Her breathing quickened and she moved her body against the dark head pressed close to her. When she thought that she could no longer fight against the need to climax he levered himself over her and their love-making, in deep, urgent thrusts, reached its pinnacle.

It was cool in the room. She only noticed it as the heated passion ebbed away, and she rolled over to her side, sat up and reached for her clothes.

'What are you doing?' He propped himself up on one elbow and looked at her lazily.

She disregarded the bra, but slung her shirt over her and slipped on her briefs.

She didn't know how she felt. Confused, elated, mixed up. Conflicting emotions were running through her with such speed that she couldn't seem to pin any one of them down.

Of course, she knew that making love with him had been an act of sheer insanity, but the bitter regret she should have felt was absent. She felt utterly complete and fulfilled, which, she thought, did nothing to repair the situation. But she didn't even know whether she wanted the situation repaired.

'It's cold in here,' she said, looking at him and wanting to reach out and stroke his face. 'I'm putting on my clothes.'

'I can light the log fire.'

'Also, I'm tired.'

He laughed throatily. 'Is that a compliment about my love-making?' Then he reached out and trailed his finger along the exposed skin under the shirt. 'Are you feeling better now?'

Leigh's hand momentarily froze, then she resumed what she had been doing—putting on her trousers.

His question had been amicable enough so why had it started alarm bells ringing in her head?

She knew that one minute ago he would have been

able to talk her into removing every item of clothing she had just put on. Now she wanted to leave.

'I feel good,' she told him, with a trace of coolness in her voice. He sat up and started to get dressed as well.

'I share the feeling.' He smiled at her and she smiled back, but it was an effort.

Did he imagine, she thought, that that little session had been some form of therapy? He had offered himself as a shoulder to cry on because he had mistakenly thought that, poor, unsophisticated child that she was, she had still been suffering from the throes of some kind of unrequited love. Had he included love-making as his show of kindness towards his daughter's poor aunt?

Now that the seed had taken root, she discovered that it was growing at a remarkable speed.

He bent to kiss her and she drew back. She felt like ice. More than that, she felt a complete fool because she had given herself to him with abandon and he had made love to her out of pity.

And what about Fiona? He had not once said that they were lovers but, on the other hand, in the face of her oblique questioning he had not denied it either.

Was he involved with the other woman?

Her instinct was to hurl her wounded anger at him, but she knew that that was something she had to keep well under control. Her position in his house was tenuous at best.

'What's the matter?' Nicholas asked sharply, sensing the change in her mood.

'Nothing.' She stood back and looked at him. 'I realise that we can't turn the clock back, but what happened just then was a mistake.'

'What?' The drowsy aftermath of making love had vanished. His eyes, as they swept over her, were hard and penetrating. She could almost feel him trying to get inside her head and work out what she was thinking, and the frightening thing was that she reckoned he could do it—prise open her mind and read her like a book. 'What do you mean—*a mistake*?'

If she hadn't known better, she thought, she might have been taken in by that look of genuine, angry perplexity on his face.

'I mean we shouldn't have made love. You're fond of telling me that I'm a child, but I'm not a child and I'm mature enough to know that what we just did was stupid. I'm your daughter's aunt and I'm here to do a job.'

'Why are you running away from me?' he demanded, his face angled and hard.

'I am not running away from you.' She laughed dismissively, but in her own ears she could hear the edge of misery beneath it. 'I just think that we have to forget what took place for Amy's sake.'

'How does Amy come into this?'

'I have no intention of embarking on some kind of affair with you. I'm not looking for an affair, and I don't expect you are either.' Considering, she thought, that you've probably got one going in full swing with Fiona. 'I don't want to complicate anything.' She turned on her heel and began to walk towards the door. He reached out and curled his fingers around her arm.

'You're talking in riddles—' he began harshly.

'I'm telling you,' she said, 'that I'm here as Amy's nanny and I have no intention of romping in the hay with you. I don't see that it's going to get either of us anywhere, and I don't think that you do either.'

'Don't tell me what I think.'

'I won't. But leave me alone from this point on.' She

didn't dare look back as she left the room. She didn't want to read the expression on his face. Most of all, she didn't want to be talked into something she knew would pose the greatest danger of all.

CHAPTER EIGHT

THE following day Nicholas told Leigh over coffee in the kitchen, that he would be away for a couple of days.

'Business,' he said, and she wondered whether she was imagining the curtness behind the word or whether she was simply over-sensitive to any nuances between them, real or otherwise, after what had happened the night before.

She had not slept well. She had retreated to bed to wallow in the memory of their love-making, going over in her head, in relentless detail, what had inspired him to touch her—attempting to analyse every snippet of conversation she could remember. In retrospect, everything had seemed imbued with innuendo.

Had he asked her to do some typing for him because he'd felt guilty that her role of nanny was so limited? A patronising title for a job that had been invented for her out of necessity? Maybe he'd thought she would feel more worthwhile under his roof if she'd thought she'd been contributing more. Had that been it? Had that been his reasoning?

Had he thought that she would accept his kind offer to do some occasional work for him because they both knew, without anything being said, that the decision-making process when it came to his daughter was steadily going into his hands now?

Or maybe he was regretting the inflated salary he had initially agreed to pay her. After all, he had needed her then, but that situation was altering daily. Maybe he felt

138

that he could get a bit more out of her by way of doing work for him.

True, he had perfunctorily offered to increase her salary if she accepted his offer, but he must have known that she would have refused any such thing had she agreed. She was paid way too much as it was for something she enjoyed doing and would have done for nothing.

Was that it? Was it? She spent hours lying on her bed, labouring at the problem, until she finally closed her eyes at a little after four-thirty, only to reawaken, bleary-eyed, at seven in the morning.

'But you will be back before Christmas Eve, won't you?' Amy stopped eating her toast to ask in an anxious voice.

'Of course I will.' His voice had softened, and Leigh felt a stab of idiotic jealousy, followed by bewilderment at her own reaction.

'Where are you going?' Leigh asked him, not quite able to meet his eyes, but not quite able either to keep her gaze totally away from him. He stood at the kitchen sink, drinking a cup of coffee, impeccably dressed for work in a charcoal grey suit. He looked depressingly refreshed.

'New York.'

Amy stopped eating completely at this and her eyes opened as wide as saucers. 'Wow!' she said, impressed, and he smiled at her. 'Will you bring me back something?'

'Amy!' Leigh said in a sharp, warning voice.

Wasn't that a clear indication of how far the relationship between father and child had developed over the weeks? She could remember the dubious suspicion with which Amy had greeted his initial present in that restaurant in Covent Garden. Now here she sat, asking him to bring her back something, with the insouciance of someone fully confident of the reaction they would get to their request. Whether Amy was aware of it or not, Nicholas had already slipped into the role of father.

'What about Santa?' he asked with a concerned frown. 'I wouldn't like to put his nose out of joint.'

'Oh, yes, that's true.' Amy carried on with the toast. 'It *is* a bit close to Christmas Day for extra presents. You could always get my present from New York,' she said coaxingly.

'Like what?'

So far, Leigh thought, Nicholas had not once looked at her. He did not appear to be ignoring her, merely indifferent, and that hurt, even though she knew that she could hardly have expected an effusive response after what had happened between them.

'A computer game?' she suggested. 'Or a costume?'

'Nicholas will be busy, working,' Leigh said gently to her niece. 'I don't think he'll have time to go shopping.'

He did look at her when she said that, a long, cold look that spoke volumes. 'Why don't you go and write me a list, Amy?' he said, still looking at Leigh. 'But be quick. I leave in about half an hour for the airport.'

Amy darted out of the kitchen, and as soon as she was out of earshot he said in a hard voice, 'Don't tell Amy what I will or will not have time to do.'

'I was not *telling* her what you will or won't have time to do!' Leigh snapped back. 'If anything, I was giving you some leeway so that you didn't commit yourself to something you might not physically be able to do.'

'How thoughtful of you.'

'Yes, I think so!' She could feel tears spring to the back of her eyes, and she concentrated on drinking some more coffee.

It was ridiculous but she had become accustomed, she now realised, to a certain lack of animosity between them. True, there was not a complete absence of tension, but the times when he had smiled, had turned on his charm, had made her laugh, more than made up for that.

She took a deep breath. 'I know you're angry with me about last night...' She had resolved not to mention it. She had been utterly determined that wild horses would not drag it out of her mouth. She would never, she had told herself the night before, refer to that episode again. So much, she thought, for her will-power.

'Angry?' He gave a short, cold laugh. 'You flatter yourself. Why should I be angry with you?'

She shrugged and miserably contemplated the dregs of the coffee in her cup.

'Well?' He had crossed the room swiftly and positioned himself in the chair next to her. Out of the corner of her eye she could see his hand on the table, and she felt a little shiver of nervousness. 'Don't make statements like that, Leigh, unless you're prepared to back them up.'

'OK. You're not angry.' It seemed the easiest way to avoid a confrontation, but her placatory voice only enraged him further.

'I didn't bring the subject up,' he told her harshly. '*You* did. So don't think that you can now shy away from the topic because you find it uncomfortable.'

'You're angry because you didn't get your own way,' she flung at him. She glanced up at his face and then looked away again to the uninteresting brown liquid, now quite cold and showing signs of cultivating a disgusting film over the surface. 'I don't know what you wanted, what you expected...'

She felt herself becoming a little bogged down. She didn't want to make sweeping assumptions about what he had expected after their love-making but, on the other hand, he was forcing her to defend the stance she had taken, and she could have kicked herself for having mentioned anything at all.

'I'm sorry that I'm not interested in cultivating an affair with you. Or even,' she added hurriedly, just in case she had misread the situation and he wasn't at all interested in anything of the sort, 'another one-night stand.'

'Because you're not that sort of girl?' His lips twisted into a cynical mimicry of a smile.

'That's right!' Leigh hissed angrily.

'You're a good, clean, home-loving kind of girl who wouldn't dream of having an affair with anyone unless there was something at the end of it.'

'I never said that...'

'Was that why your relationship with that boyfriend of yours hit the rocks? Never mind about him being unable to accept responsibility. Did you offer him the ultimatum of marriage or out?'

'I did nothing of the kind! And I have no idea what that has to do with...what happened between us.'

'Maybe nothing. Maybe everything. Tell me, Leigh, what *was* last night all about? I'm mystified by a woman who could lie moaning in my arms one minute, and then spring to her feet, stick all her clothes back on and announce that it's all been a terrible mistake.'

And I'm mystified by a man who could sleep with a woman because he feels sorry for her. She wondered, viciously, whether he was even physically attracted to her at all. She supposed he must have been, just for an instant, or maybe he had just accepted what had been so blatantly on offer.

'I came to my senses,' she said defensively.

'And what made you lose them in the first place?'

She stared at him, unable to say anything to that remark, and was saved having to think of something by Amy, who re-entered the kitchen, bearing a sheet of paper copiously covered with her neat, joined-up, childish writing.

'Just a few things,' Amy said, handing Nicholas the sheet of paper, which Leigh could read upside down. There were brackets qualifying nearly all the entries, and rambling explanations of precisely what was meant by what. She would have smiled at it all if she had been in any mood for smiling.

'Well,' Nicholas said gravely, standing up and slipping on his jacket which had been lying on the central island in the kitchen, 'I'll see what I can do. Of course, I shall have to consult with Santa just to make sure that we don't duplicate presents.'

'Course,' Amy said, grinning, 'although I never knew that he was in the phone book.'

Leigh stood as well and folded her arms. 'And will you be contactable...while you're in New York?'

He gave her a curt, unrevealing look and scribbled the name of a hotel and a telephone number on a piece of paper. 'I'll leave it here, shall I?' He bent and planted a kiss on the top of his daughter's head, then he rumpled her hair, laughing as she frantically smoothed it back into shape. 'And I'll see you,' he addressed Amy, 'in two days' time. Be good.'

'I'm always good.'

'Especially before Christmas,' Leigh joked feebly, noticing how he ignored her completely.

The house felt empty as soon as he had gone. They went out to do a bit of Christmas shopping, but there was no real anticipation for Leigh at the prospect of returning to an empty house.

She remained cheerful for Amy's sake, but it was difficult, especially as part of their Christmas shopping included the purchase of gifts for Nicholas from Amy—a stuffed toy, of all things, a book and a bright red tie with Mickey Mouse all over it.

'I can't see him wearing that,' Leigh said, raising her eyebrows, but her niece insisted. It was fun, she said, nicer than those boring things he wore to work.

'What are *you* going to buy him?' Amy asked, and Leigh, who had only given the matter surface thought, frowned and wondered what she could possibly get for a man who now had nothing whatsoever to say to her.

She shrugged and said, 'A jumper, I guess.' It was as impersonal as she could get, without resorting to socks and handkerchiefs.

'Can I choose it?'

'Why not?' That meant she ended up with a jumper bearing the improbable motif of a family of teddy bears. A less likely jumper for Nicholas Kendall would have been hard to come by.

She maintained a pretence of simmering excitement over the next day as she and Amy wrapped presents and distributed them to their few friends, who now seemed to belong to another life completely.

It seemed as though she had known Nicholas Kendall all her life, and she would have bet money that Amy felt the same way as well. How on earth could someone get under her skin so comprehensively and with such speed?

She was curled up in the sitting room with her book, half reading, half letting her thoughts drift to Nicholas, before reining them in, when she heard someone walking towards the room.

Her immediate thought was that it was Nicholas, and her heart began to beat a little faster. He wasn't due to arrive until the following evening, but maybe he had done whatever he had gone to New York to do and was returning early.

She made an effort to compose her features into a mask of politeness, and was baring her teeth into a semblance of a smile when she saw Fiona, standing at the door, and her heart sank. She felt disappointment and alarm at having to converse with the woman. It had been optimistic to think that she could see Christmas through, without Fiona appearing on the scene somewhere along the line.

'Hi,' she said unenthusiastically. She took one last, lingering look at her book and shut it.

Fiona walked into the room with the self-assurance of someone so accustomed to stealing the limelight that the talent was now embedded, regardless of the audience in question.

She was wearing a luxurious fur coat, real or fake Leigh had no way of telling, which she deposited on a chair. Then she sat down, crossed her long legs and said coolly, 'I had hoped to find you here.'

'Can I get you something to drink?' The question was motivated less by politeness than by the need to find a temporary escape.

'I'll have a gin and tonic, I think.' On the arms of the chair her hands were perfectly still. 'Considering it's Christmas. Only sociable to have a drink with the hired help—don't you agree?'

The remark was designed to cut, and Leigh rose to her feet, refusing to let herself be undermined. She had enough troubles on her plate, without adding to the stress.

Instead, without saying anything, she poured Fiona her drink, handed it to her and returned to her chair.

'Now, Fiona, I can tell that you haven't come here so that we can make polite conversation about the weather, and we both know that Nicholas is away, so why don't you just get to the point and say what you have to say?'

'Call a spade a spade,' Fiona said thoughtfully, sipping her drink. 'Such directness. I'll bet that your relatives stem from up North somewhere.'

Leigh didn't think that her family tree was on the menu either, and she allowed that remark to pass as well. 'I haven't seen you around much lately,' she said finally. 'Busy at work?' If Fiona wanted to beat around the bush then she could play that game as well.

'Rushed off my feet,' Fiona answered coldly. 'Which is more than I can say about you. You certainly landed on yours, didn't you?'

'Nicholas has been very generous, yes.'

'That's something of an understatement. You're being paid, as I understand it, to look after your niece.'

Leigh didn't say anything. She didn't care for the way the conversation was going but she had no idea how to change its direction.

'What are you trying to say, Fiona?' she asked eventually.

'I'm trying to say that one minute you're on the brink of bankruptcy and the next minute you're living in the lap of luxury, and relishing every minute of it, no doubt.'

'I never asked Nicholas to take us in. He volunteered, and I had no choice.'

'Or, rather, you chose not to exercise it.'

'Look, I'm sorry if my presence here has...disturbed whatever you and Nicholas had going...'

'Oh, I'm sure.' She swigged another mouthful of her drink. In a minute she would have finished it, and in record time. Leigh hoped that she wasn't the sort who became aggressive after alcohol.

'You're not sorry at all,' Fiona expanded, demolishing the remnants of her drink in one gulp and then getting up to pour herself another—twice as strong, from the looks of it. 'You're an opportunist, little Miss Nanny, and I don't intend to see all my plans thrown to the four corners of the earth because of you.'

'Plans? What plans?'

Fiona returned to her chair—fully composed, Leigh was thankful to see.

'My family and Nick's go back a long way,' she said with a tight, hard smile. 'My parents would like nothing better than to see us happily married. Why on earth do you think I'm staying here?'

'You're planning on getting married?' She had a momentary vision of a large white wedding, with Amy as bridesmaid, and her peering in from behind the gates. She began to perspire lightly.

'Things were moving along nicely until you and that little brat came on the scene. Nicholas and I have everything in common. We come from the same world, my dear. Where do *you* come from?' Fiona paused only to draw breath. 'We both enjoy life in the fast lane. He may be happy now, playing at being a daddy, but the novelty of that will wear off soon enough.'

'He told you about his relationship to Amy?'

'He didn't have to,' Fiona said contemptuously. 'It's obvious to anyone with half a brain. You just need to

look at the two of them to see the resemblance and—
let's face it—why else would he have given you shelter?
I know she's not *your* child. I've heard her address you
as Auntie so I can only imagine that your sister, wherever she might be, is the mother.'

'Look, I'm tired, Fiona...and I don't know where any
of this is leading.'

'I won't leave here without a fight—do you understand me?'

'Leave?'

'That's right. As if you didn't know. Nicholas feels
that it's time I found a place of my own. I can only
surmise from that that you and he are sleeping together,
and it's more convenient for you both to have me out
of the way.'

'You're way out of line!' Leigh half stood, white-
faced.

'Are you sleeping together?'

'No, we are not!' One occasion did not warrant the
description of sleeping together, did it? And, anyway,
she had no obligation to tell Fiona anything.

But what, she wondered, was the real story here? Had
Nicholas been sleeping with Fiona before? Had he given
her her walking papers because he assumed that she,
Leigh, would be happy enough to take up where Fiona
left off? Maybe he fancied the change. As Fiona had
said, she and Nicholas had everything in common,
whereas what did she, Leigh, have in common with him?
He was a wealthy, ambitious, fast-living businessman.
She was an artist whose idea of wealth had always meant
a trip to the movies followed by a cheap Italian somewhere in Shepherd's Bush. Her sister and Roy had been
comfortable enough in their heyday but, even then, they
were vastly outstripped by the likes of Nicholas Kendall.

No, Fiona was right. Two worlds had temporarily collided, and would soon move out of each other's orbit.

'Well, just think twice before you do anything, my dear. I'm sure your little niece has no idea who her real father is. You wouldn't want her to find out, would you? Might be quite a shock to her system, wouldn't you say? Might destroy all the trust you two have taken such pains to develop.' Fiona stood up and brushed down her skirt, which was short, black and expensive.

'I might be out of this house, but I have no intention of being out of Nicholas's life, and believe me when I tell you that you're no match for me.' She slipped on her fur coat, which seemed designed for someone of Fiona's tall, slender proportions. She walked towards the door, paused and looked over her shoulder, 'Merry Christmas, by the way.' Then she was gone. Leigh waited until the sound of muffled footsteps faded, then she made her way up to bed.

Well, what next? she thought. A snake under the bed? A couple of letter bombs from an unknown admirer? Could Christmas get any more stressed than it already was?

On top of having this little jaunt in the countryside to look forward to, where she and Nicholas would treat each other with freezing politeness, only smiling for the sake of Amy, she now had a head full of Fiona's threats and malice to contend with as well.

She went to sleep with the onset of a headache, and awoke the following morning feeling no better than when she had gone to bed.

Amy's excitement level was now running at an all-time high, although she was trying hard to maintain some semblance of nonchalance because she imagined that that would have been the attitude of most of the friends in her class.

There were a fair number of phone calls made to these friends, however, and Leigh was amused to see that nonchalance seemed to be quite low on the agenda.

She managed to retire to bed before Nicholas arrived, although when she woke up in the middle of the night she couldn't help feeling as though the house was suddenly alive again, knowing that he was back home.

There were traces of his return when she went downstairs the following morning as well—American newspapers on the kitchen table, loose currency lying in a careless pile on one of the counters, his tie draped over the banister where he had presumably left it *en route* to his bedroom the night before.

But the man himself was nowhere to be seen. He had left early for work, she supposed, though admittedly it was after nine by the time she and Amy made their way downstairs.

This time last year, she thought, Christmas had been altogether different. It had been the first Christmas without Roy and Jenny, a fairly sombre occasion only slightly alleviated by their friends' determination to make them have as jolly a time as possible.

This time around Amy was a different child. She had made the odd wistful remark about her mum, and a couple of times Leigh had found her staring thoughtfully out of the window, but the haunted, lost look which had been so apparent the year before was gone. She had not forgotten her parents, but she was remembering what it was like to look forward again.

What if Fiona carried out her threat to tell Amy about Nicholas?

Leigh uneasily suspected that the threat was an idle

one. Fiona was going to be off the scene from now on and, besides, she and Nicholas would tell Amy themselves in due course as soon as Christmas was out of the way and school had settled into a pleasant routine.

All thoughts of Fiona and her threats faded as evening approached, to be replaced by the nervous anticipation of seeing Nicholas again.

He seemed to have that effect on her. It was as if his intrusion in her head was so immense that there was literally no room for anything else. She hardly gave a thought to college the following term, to Fiona or to whatever the future had in store.

When she finally saw him that night, just as she was about to settle down next to Amy in her bedroom to listen to another chapter from her spooky children's book, she was struck by his forcefulness all over again.

He walked into the room, after briefly knocking, still in his working clothes, although minus his tie, which was probably hanging over the banister in the hall. He looked tired, but that seemed to disappear as soon as he set eyes on his daughter.

From the sidelines Leigh watched as he chatted to Amy as he sat on the side of the bed, depressing it with his weight, listening to Amy's elaborate recounting of how they had spent their past couple of days. Under Nicholas's amused eyes Amy blossomed from an attractive child into a radiant one. Her face became animated, her eyes glowed and her laughter, which was something bestowed upon only the deserving, was infectious.

Whatever her own fate might turn out to be, watching the two of them together, Leigh knew that it had all been worthwhile—the doubts about contacting him, his suspicion about her motives, his accusations and the coolness which had now settled between them like a glacier.

It gave her a bitter-sweet sense of satisfaction.

When Amy was finally tucked up Leigh headed in the opposite direction to Nicholas towards the studio where she intended to spend a couple of hours attempting to do something with the painting she had been working on for the past three weeks, but she heard him say from behind her, 'Not so fast, Leigh. I want to have a word with you.'

She stopped in her tracks and reluctantly turned. What about? she wanted to ask. Instead, she said, as cheerfully as possible, 'Sure.' She followed him down the stairs, amused, despite herself, to see his tie precisely where she had expected it to be.

'We need to do something with the presents,' he told her, turning to look at her.

'Oh, we've wrapped all ours already.'

'We need to put them in the boot of the car. We won't get the chance to do it in the morning, not without Amy prancing around, peering into everything.'

'OK!' She felt quite proud of her composure. No one would have guessed that the mere sight of him was making her head swim.

It took longer than she had expected, the fetching and carrying of the presents from the cupboard in her bedroom into black bin liners. Aside from a vast assortment of gifts which Nicholas had bought, he had also bought Amy a bicycle, which Leigh stepped back to look at.

'Very impressive,' she said, folding her arms. 'You've certainly taken this present-buying business to new heights.'

Nicholas seemed nonplussed by that. 'I have no idea what she's been…accustomed to…' he said eventually.

'It wasn't meant to be a criticism.' Just in case, she thought, he decided to embark on an argument over it.

She had decided that whatever had happened between the two of them she was not going to allow any of it to spoil Amy's Christmas.

She hovered by the open front door and shivered in her long, comfortable black skirt and T-shirt, watching as he loaded the boot. She remained with her arms folded as he slammed the front door behind him when it was all done.

'Well,' she said brightly, 'that's done now. Was there…anything else…?' She sounded like a congenial interviewer, hoping to wrap up a tiresome interview.

'How about a cup of coffee?' he suggested, his hands in his pockets.

This was hardly what she had expected. Coldness, yes. Distance, yes. A few curt monosyllables and the odd cutting remark. Certainly not this show of courtesy, far less the awkwardness that seemed to accompany it. She wondered whether he had similarly arrived at the conclusion that any disagreements between them should be put to rest, at least over the Christmas break.

'Why not?' Leigh said, with a shrug.

She had become so accustomed to the workings of his kitchen that once there she automatically began to make the coffee. Proper, fresh coffee, if only because he produced the packet from the larder, leaving her little choice in the matter.

'You can get the cups,' she said, and poured boiling water into the cafetière, not bothering to look around at him. 'They're in the cupboard above the Aga,' she added, after he had opened and shut a few doors.

It was hardly surprising that he did not know the exact locations of most of the things he possessed. As a bachelor, she doubted whether he ever used his kitchen. Mrs MacBride prepared food for him during the day if he was expected to eat at home in the evening, but most evenings, she suspected, he spent out.

He handed her two mugs, which she filled with coffee. They sat at the kitchen table, drinking and discussing what time they would set off the following day and how long the trip would take. She asked him about New York, and whether he had accomplished what he had set out to do. It was all very civilised, she thought. It was amazing what can be concealed under a veneer of politeness.

In a minute she would finish her coffee, excuse herself—safe in the knowledge that she had behaved with decorum—and go up to bed. In the morning there would be more of the same. And the morning after, and the morning after that. All those mornings, crammed full of civilised behaviour, until the time came for her to say goodbye and leave, whenever that might be, and she would depart in a similarly civilised manner.

Underneath, her heart was pounding and her thoughts were doing wild somersaults in her head.

She looked at him surreptitiously, taking in his dark good looks, the way his long fingers curled around his mug and the glimpse of chest where he had unbuttoned the top of his shirt after he had removed his tie.

'Right, then,' she said, rising, 'I guess I'd better be off to bed now if I'm to get up on time tomorrow. Not that there's much chance of Amy letting me have a lie-in.' She walked towards the kitchen sink, tipped out the contents of her mug and rinsed it.

'I've been thinking about you,' he said lazily, and she stiffened.

'Oh?' She turned very slowly, folded her arms and leaned against the counter.

He stretched out his legs and continued to look at her

speculatively, his head a little tilted to one side, as though listening for the meaning behind her words.

'Thinking about what happened between us, and you know exactly what I'm talking about. I'm talking about what we've been at great pains this evening to pretend never took place.' His eyes were brooding, mesmerising.

'I'm not pretending anything,' Leigh began shakily, clearing her throat because the distance between them seemed like a million miles. She felt as though she had to shout to make herself heard. 'It was a mistake.'

'Why?'

'Because...'

'That's no kind of answer. You said that you had come to your senses, that it was all a terrible mistake, but I think that you're afraid.'

'Afraid of what?'

'Afraid of what you feel when I touch you.'

How could he say that in such an apparently normal voice? When she heard him she felt as though she were being systematically stripped, all her essentials laid bare for his inspection.

'I think you want me, and you find that so overwhelming that your instinct is to run away from it, to pretend that it doesn't exist, that it's something that can be controlled.'

There *was* a response to that. Leigh knew there was if only she could gather her wits and get her vocal chords to work.

'I'm here as a nanny...' she said almost inaudibly, 'I don't want to compromise...Amy... We both have to consider...'

'This has nothing to do with compromise.' His voice was hypnotic. He stood up very calmly and strolled over to where she was still leaning rigidly against the worktop. 'This has nothing to do with your position here. This has nothing to do with the fact that you work for me. This,' he said, and he was standing right in front of her now, 'has to do with something far more elemental than that.'

'Why?' She looked at him with a trace of desperation in her eyes. 'Why are you pursuing this? Why can't you just leave it alone? Is it because you feel that you have to get every woman you want? Is this to do with your pride?'

'Pride has nothing to do with anything,' he said softly. When he raised his hand and ran one finger along the side of her face she felt her skin begin to burn. 'And, believe it or not, I don't go through life, assuming that it's my right to conquer the female race. Nor am I some monstrous rampant male who can't survive without a woman in my bed.'

Leigh wondered what sort of sight she presented with her mouth half open and her eyes wide—a zombie.

'The plain truth of the matter,' he murmured, 'is that I want you. No, that's not strictly true. I *crave* you.' He traced the line of her collarbone, then, over her T-shirt, followed the contours of her breasts. 'And I wouldn't be doing this now,' he said, his voice low and unsteady, 'if I didn't believe that you felt the same way. If you don't then tell me, and this will never happen again.'

In that instant, with his words hovering in the air between them, Leigh made her decision. No more fighting. Let fate and time do their worst, but this physical thing was too strong. It leapt across the barriers between them, made nonsense of her reasoning, threw her life into turmoil.

She closed her eyes and raised her lips to his, and as his mouth met hers she arched her body against him and kissed him with feverish abandon. This thing inside her—only he could satisfy it, and she would let him.

His hands circled her waist and slipped underneath her T-shirt. She hitched it up and undid her bra from behind, freeing her breasts for his touch.

Her nipples ached and she pushed his hands to them, groaning as he massaged her breasts. When he lowered his head to suck the throbbing peaks she pushed her fingers into his hair and pressed him against her. His tongue, flicking across her nipples, sent waves of pleasure surging through every pore of her body.

Neither of them heard footsteps. Neither of them heard the sharp intake of breath. Their passion drowned out all sound. It was only when Leigh opened her eyes that she realised that they were no longer alone.

CHAPTER NINE

LEIGH jumped back, shocked at the sight of Fiona. She desperately tried to arrange herself into some semblance of order, which only increased her feeling of discomposure.

'Well, well, well.' Fiona strolled into the kitchen, and Nicholas turned and looked at her. Leigh, who wanted to get as much distance between them as possible, had retreated to the Aga, where she now stood with her trembling hands tightly clasped behind her back.

'Hello, Fiona,' Nicholas said, and his mouth parted in a cold smile. 'What are you doing here?'

'Actually, I dropped in to give you a Christmas present.' She produced a beautifully wrapped box and deposited it with a thud on the kitchen counter. For the first time since Leigh had met her she was wearing a pair of jeans, immaculately tailored, with flat, tan-coloured loafers and an off-white cashmere jumper tucked into the jeans. Her blonde hair wasn't tied back, but hung in a rich, velvety curtain to her shoulders.

She folded her arms, gave Leigh a cursory glance and then half turned her body so that she was facing Nicholas.

'I might have guessed that there was a reason you wanted me out of your house so quickly.'

Nicholas narrowed his eyes and looked at the blonde. 'You're entitled to think whatever you like, Fiona,' he said quietly. His face was hard but his voice, when he spoke, was perfectly modulated.

Standing there, by the Aga, on the sidelines, Leigh felt completely excluded from what was taking place between the two of them. She was a spectator, but a spectator to a scene not meant for her eyes. If only there had been some way out of the kitchen she would have left, but there wasn't. Not without walking right between them, and that was the last thing she wanted to do.

'How could you!' Fiona took an involuntary step forward. 'I thought—'

'What? What did you think, Fiona?'

'We've known each other a long time, Nicholas...'

Leigh heard that and for some reason she felt a shiver of uncontrollable envy as she imagined them growing up together—going to the same parties, playing with the same friends, bonding on the same level. No wonder Fiona had pointed out how ridiculous it was to think that she and Nicholas could ever have anything in common.

There certainly was no way that she could visualise what it must have been like to grow up alongside Nicholas Kendall. His childhood would have been spent, no doubt, roaming the grounds of his parents' country estate, riding horses when the weather was fine and jetting off to sunny climes with his parents in winter.

What had she been doing at a similar age? Her childhood had been a stable and happy one, but the birthday cakes had all been home-made, the holidays had all been in Britain and the school uniforms had all been handed down.

As a teenager, he would have already been moving forward to his eventual life in the fast lane, cosseted by money, protected from possible failure.

'Which is why I'm standing here, having this conversation with you, Fiona. Because there's absolutely no reason why I should have to justify myself or my actions

to you—or to anyone else, for that matter.' His very lack
of emotion was dramatic. There was a certain intimidat-
ing, contained power in his stillness.

Leigh was pretty sure that they had both forgotten her
presence. Now she wondered whether she couldn't simply hide somewhere in the kitchen, maybe sidle towards
the door that led to the utility room and take refuge
behind it.

'I thought when you agreed that I could come here—'

'That I was agreeing to more than just providing some
temporary accommodation?'

'Why not?' she threw at him. 'I recall a time when
you couldn't get enough of my company!'

'Years ago, Fiona,' he told her patiently. 'A fling,
that's all. You moved on with your career, went abroad,
travelled the world.'

So, Leigh thought, her stomach twisting, they *had* had
a relationship. Whether it happened yesterday or ten
years ago, they had still touched one another, been close.
She had to tell herself not to be ridiculous. She hadn't
imagined that he had lived a life of self-imposed celi-
bacy, had she? Of course he had had relationships with
women. But had he loved Fiona? Did he love her now,
without realising it?

'Look...' He shifted his position slightly, transferring
weight from one leg to the other. 'When my mother
telephoned me and asked whether I would put you up I
was more than happy to oblige. You're right. We go
back a long way.'

'And we can keep on going, Nicholas!' She stretched
out her hands in an urgent gesture, then allowed them
to fall to her sides. 'We were made for one another!
Have you considered that? I think our parents have al-

ways…expected us to perhaps end up with each other…and why not? We have a lot in common!'

'Less than you imagine, Fiona.' He seemed neither amused nor persuaded by her argument.

Leigh gave an exploratory little cough on the off-chance that it might stall this intimate conversation and provide an opportunity for her to leave. She had no wish to hear all this, no desire to go down memory lane with them. Neither of them paid her the slightest bit of attention.

For a minute, she indulged in a frightful thought. What if Fiona, with her very sensible arguments, won the day? She was a beautiful woman. That alone would have been enough for most men. What if she made Nicholas see what was apparently obvious to her—and pretty obvious to Leigh as well when she thought about it?

What if she was forced to witness them putting aside their differences, their arms around one another, in an embrace that would last a lifetime?

'But more than you have with some…' She glanced around at Leigh and Nicholas followed the direction of her gaze.

'This has nothing to do with Leigh.'

'On the contrary, this has *everything* to do with her.'

'I would rather you two didn't conduct your conversation around me,' Leigh said icily. This was the opportunity she had been waiting for and she made a move to walk past them, but she didn't get very far.

'Where are you going?' Nicholas asked, staring at her. She returned his stare defiantly.

'Up to my room. I really don't think I need to be here, listening to all of this. If you two want to have your little tiff, then leave me out of it!'

There was petulance, disappointment and downright jealousy in her voice, but she couldn't control it. She could barely meet Nicholas's eyes.

'Stay!' It was a command, and it brought her to a complete stop.

'I want to know what's going on between the two of you,' Fiona said harshly, and Nicholas gave her a look of such scorn that she continued hurriedly, 'Whatever it is, it won't last, Nicholas. Use your head! She's an opportunist! Can't you see that?'

'That's not true!' Leigh spluttered angrily.

'I think it's time for you to leave, Fiona,' Nicholas said, and she shook her head vehemently.

'Not until you've heard me out!'

When he looked as though he had no intention of doing any such thing she drew back, shaking her head, her fingers digging into her arms.

'You owe me that at least!'

'What the hell makes you think that?'

'Because we share a past!'

'We grew up together, in a manner of speaking, Fiona. I wouldn't really call that sharing a past.'

But his stance had softened. He felt sorry for Fiona, Leigh thought with surprise. He was reluctant to hurt her.

How, she wondered, did that make Fiona feel? Leigh's mind shot ahead to a time when he got bored with her, bored with her accessibility, when he felt sorry for her, too, and the thought of that made her feel a little sick.

'She's not right for you,' Fiona said, slipping back into the mode of speaking about Leigh as though she wasn't, in fact, standing only a few feet away.

'Not *right* for me?' He looked a little bemused by that

statement, as though the conversation had taken an unexpected twist.

'She doesn't belong in your world,' Fiona told him in the voice of someone driving a point home.

'Let me put you straight on a couple of things, Fiona.' There was no amusement in his voice now. 'The first is that I don't give a damn about whether someone comes from the same background as me or not. Because that's what you're talking about, isn't it? Do you imagine for a minute that having a similar background is a foolproof route to lifelong love and commitment?' He gave a short, mirthless laugh.

'And the second is this—you seem to think that marriage is the be all and end all of all relationships. I'm not in the process of searching for my ideal mate.'

Leigh felt the colour drain out of her face. He was only saying what she had known all along, but still the words cut into her like a knife. She reached behind her and gripped the edge of the kitchen counter.

'I hope you hear that!' Fiona turned to her with an expression of triumph on her face. 'What a blow for you! I expect you imagined that you could just jump into bed with him and then two days later you would be walking into Asprey's to choose the engagement ring!'

'I never thought any such thing,' Leigh whispered.

'That's enough!' Nicholas barked. 'I want you out of here now, Fiona! When it comes to marriage I assure you that you never even entered the list of candidates.'

Fiona's face went a mottled shade of red. 'Suit yourself! But you'll be sorry, Nicholas Kendall. How do you think your parents are going to feel when they're confronted by their one and only son with his illegitimate child? I'll bet you haven't mentioned a word about that daughter of yours!' She laughed and it wasn't a pleasant sound.

'I'd advise you not to meddle in things that don't concern you, Fiona,' he said in a hard voice.

'Or else what?' She began to walk out of the kitchen. 'The thought of seeing their faces when I tell them that you're a father...'

'Leave now before I do something I regret.' He hadn't raised his voice, but it still carried the intensity of a whiplash. With one last look, Fiona swept out of the kitchen, leaving behind her a heavy, uncomfortable silence.

'I really think it's time I went to bed,' Leigh said eventually, and he nodded.

'I'll see you in the morning.' He looked at her and then turned away completely so that he was leaning against the counter, propped against it by his hands, with his head lowered.

Thinking what?

Leigh escaped before he had a chance to turn around. She just wanted to get out of the kitchen, out of his presence, as quickly as she could.

She was shaking all over as she got to her bedroom, and she had to force herself to calm down and take a few deep long breaths.

Why was she so upset? Hadn't it been obvious that nothing had happened between Nicholas and Fiona? Shouldn't that have made her happy? At least she hadn't had to deal with the possibility of being the eager lover on the side, the temporary distraction.

And now Fiona had left. That alone should have been cause for rejoicing. She settled under the quilt and stared up at the ceiling, which she could just make out as her eyes became acclimatised to the darkness. She told herself that one great worry was off her mind. There was no threat now that Nicholas and Fiona were destined to become some happy family unit, with Amy stuck in the middle.

Hadn't she been worried about that happening? Hadn't she imagined boarding schools and finishing schools and an end product which bore no resemblance to the child Leigh wanted Amy to be?

Shouldn't she be thrilled?

She didn't feel thrilled. She felt vaguely relieved that certain areas of stress had been removed, but beyond that she felt numb inside.

It was only as she was beginning, finally, to drift into sleep that thoughts which had been lying at the back of her mind began to stir into life and take shape.

He wasn't interested in marriage. He didn't want commitment. He wasn't particularly bothered whether she was right for him or wrong for him or neither because all he wanted out of her was sex. He had said as much to Fiona.

But I want more than that!

That grim realisation beckoned maliciously to her. Leigh had never contemplated anything with Mick, whose memory now seemed so distant that it was almost like trying to remember a long ago dream, but with Nicholas it was different.

And she had no idea when it had started to get different, no idea when things had subtly changed—when the stimulation she felt in his company had become need, when awareness had turned into attraction and attraction had turned into love.

When had that happened? How could it have happened, without her even realising it at the time?

She opened her eyes and accepted the horrifying truth.

She had somehow fallen in love with Nicholas Kendall. She couldn't imagine a less suitable candidate for her love.

Was it a surprise that she had found it impossible to visualise life without him? The times when she had told herself that Amy would get older, would accept Nicholas as her father, would no longer need her around and that she, Leigh, would once more have her freedom to do as she liked had filled her with stomach-churning nausea, and now she understood why. She didn't *want* her freedom.

So, what now? Love and marriage was not an option, and she could hardly walk out of the house, leaving Amy behind.

Her head was spinning with unanswered questions by the time she finally got to sleep. It seemed like five minutes later that she felt herself being shaken, and she opened one eye to see Amy, fully dressed and raring to go, standing by the bed.

Eight-thirty. She hadn't even finished packing! Clothes into the suitcase, toothbrushes, make-up, shoes, a book for Amy to read on the journey.

It was after nine by the time she made it downstairs, to find Nicholas ready and waiting for them.

'I had to wake her up!' Amy said incredulously, as though sleeping in on such a day was beyond the realms of human understanding.

'I was exhausted.' Leigh looked directly at Nicholas when she said this, and he returned her look, without blinking.

'It was an exhausting evening.'

She felt as though they were circling each other, trying to gauge what sort of emotions were lying at the surface after Fiona's intrusion the night before.

'Absolutely.' How can I give him up? I need him with every ounce of my body, and when it's all over and done with then I shall move on, but I can't walk away now. She smiled hesitantly. 'I hope I never have an evening like that again.'

'I think,' he said, bending to pick up her suitcase then ushering them out of the front door, 'that can be arranged.'

'How long will it take us to get there?' Amy looked up at them.

'Oh, a couple of hours,' Nicholas said, opening the passenger door for Amy to slide in, 'if we don't get stuck in snow.'

'Snow!'

'Yes,' he said gravely. 'That white stuff that Londoners only really glimpse on Christmas cards.'

He deposited the suitcase in the boot and they set off. He continued to thrill Amy with accounts of blizzards and snowstorms, which made it sound as though they were setting off on an expedition to the Antarctic.

'I hope for your sake that it snows at least once while we're there,' Leigh told him when Amy had drifted into a light doze in the back seat, 'or your credibility will be at an all-time low.'

'Yes, well.' He looked sideways at her and smiled. 'I'll just have to see what I can do.'

Leigh relaxed and told herself that there was nothing more she could expect, and that she should be happy with what she had—Amy, contented in the back seat, the man she loved sitting next to her and, at least for the moment, a certain joy in an ongoing relationship.

She could feel herself beginning to nod off when he said quietly, 'About last night...'

Her eyes flew open. 'What about last night?' she

asked cautiously. She decided that she had better get accustomed to this—to the chill that ran through her whenever his voice seemed to herald bad news, to her defences coming into operation at the slightest hint that the axe was about to fall. Wasn't this what unrequited love was all about? Weren't these the classic symptoms?

'Fiona was out of line,' he began, and Leigh hurriedly brushed his explanation aside.

'She was disappointed,' Leigh said. 'She had hoped for something more. It's not unnatural.' She paused, then continued quickly, before he could read anything into that statement, 'I mean, some women set their hearts, I guess, on marrying someone, or at least on having a long-term relationship with them, and it's a blow when things don't work out along those lines.'

Nicholas didn't reply to that immediately, and Leigh peered behind her to make sure that Amy was asleep and not listening in to what was being said. She was.

'And that's never happened to you?' he asked conversationally, and she laughed.

'Thank heavens!' She hoped the timbre of her voice carried the right note.

He didn't say anything. Busy concentrating on the roads, she assumed.

'I suppose,' he said, in the same casual voice, 'you're still too young to be planning ahead to things like marriage, settling down.'

'I suppose so!'

'The right man will come along,' he told her, with a certain amount of paternalistic amusement, which got on her nerves, even though she refused to let him see it. 'Sweep you off your feet.'

'Who knows?'

'Love works that way,' he mused, 'so I've heard.'

Since there seemed nowhere to go from there, she allowed a little silence to fall between them, then she said curiously, 'Was Fiona right? When she said that you haven't told your parents about...you know...A?'

'I haven't told them, no.'

'Why not?' Leigh asked bluntly, suddenly aware that she was spoiling for an argument. Whenever she thought about how she felt towards him, and how he felt towards her, she wanted to rant and rave. She wanted to lash out at him, all the more so because him not loving her was not something over which he had any control.

Strangely enough, from the set line of his mouth he appeared to be in a similarly foul mood. 'I'll tell them when I'm ready.'

'And when will that be? You make a great song and dance about me getting my schedules right and yet you apparently don't see fit to do the same.'

'Drop it, Leigh.'

'No.' She allowed a polite pause. 'No, I don't think I will. Do you communicate with them at all?'

'Of course I communicate with them!'

'Could you try and keep it down?' she whispered. 'Amy's sleeping!'

He shot her a look of pure frustration.

'Now, you were saying?' she said.

'Domineering woman,' he muttered under his breath, and, without thinking, Leigh said, 'Well, someone has to be, with you!'

A slow flush crept into her face and she waited for him to tell her, in that cold voice which he could summon up on occasion, the he took orders from no one, but instead he said grudgingly, 'We don't have a particularly close relationship, as it happens. We're friends, I suppose, but we only see each other three times a year or so, and then we're always on our best behaviour.'

'Why is that?'

'Are you cross-examining me?' he asked, with a hint of boyish petulance in his voice, of which, she was certain, he wasn't aware.

'I am, as a matter of fact. Why don't you have a close relationship with your parents?'

'Boarding school. I was sent away at seven.'

'Poor thing. I can't imagine Amy—'

'Absolutely not. I would never do the same with any…offspring of mine…'

'It'll come as a shock,' she told him.

'Which is why I've been putting it off, I suppose. Also, it's only fair that…' he glanced over into the back seat '…knows the full situation first…'

'Yes, I guess so.' She wondered what his parents were like. He wasn't close to them and they approved of Fiona as a suitable wife. The two things did not endear them to her.

What, she wondered, would they make of *her*? The wrong side of the tracks would take on a whole new meaning, that was for sure. But she had nothing to fear, as far as meeting them was concerned, because there would never be an introduction.

She looked out of the window, wrapped up suddenly with her thoughts, and saw that they were leaving London behind them.

By the time Amy woke up they were on the motorway, with the crowded streets of London way behind them.

Nicholas, who had seemed as lost in his own thoughts as she had been in hers, began to chat to his daughter, describing his house in the country and smiling at her detailed questions. How many rooms? How big were they? Why were there two staircases when one would do?

Intermittently Leigh joined in, slowly letting the tension out of her body. From his descriptions of this country house she had mentally revised her initial idea of what it would be like, but she was still shocked when, an hour and a half after they had set off, the car swept off the road and finally entered between two concrete pillars to draw up in front of a mansion. The place stretched away, as though unwilling to end. She struggled to imagine how many rooms there were behind the innumerable windows.

Amy had spilled out of the car, and then any chance to appreciate the house was lost in the general chaos of bags being carried to the front door and introductions to his two live-in staff who had prepared the rooms, cooked a meal and made sure that the place was warm. There was lots of fussing over Amy, and although no remarks were made she saw them look at one another and she could read what was going through their minds.

Then bags were taken up to the bedrooms—sumptuous bedrooms, colour co-ordinated from the curtains to the towels in the adjoining bathrooms.

Somewhere along the line Nicholas said to her with a smile, 'Well, what do you think?'

'I think,' Leigh replied tartly, 'that a poor bumpkin like myself could get lost in here.'

'I shall just have to make sure that that doesn't happen, then, won't I?' The warmth of the suggestion behind his words sent a little thrill of pleasure racing down her spine.

'Perhaps you could draw me a map,' she suggested.

He said with a chuckle, 'With all passages leading to my bedroom.'

Her feet didn't seem to touch the ground until much later that evening when the three of them were in the sitting room, which was smaller and cosier than the formal drawing rooms—of which there were more than one—and in which the Christmas tree had been put up.

It was a gigantic affair, stretching to the tall ceiling. Amy scurried around the bottom, attaching ornaments in a fairly random fashion, while Nicholas stood on a ladder and attached ones higher up in a similarly random fashion

'You're both putting too many on the right-hand side,' Leigh complained from where she was sitting on the ground, having been relegated to the more lowly job of sticking hooks through the ornaments. 'The tree's beginning to look lopsided.' Father and daughter looked at her with identical expressions of bewilderment.

'And you're not distributing the colours evenly enough. Too many ivory ones on that branch. And that angel at the top...' She shook her head. 'Is she all right? I mean, she's leaning over as though she's had too much to drink.' Which Amy found hysterically funny.

If only this could go on for ever, Leigh thought, the banter, the feeling of peaceful companionship. The illusion of perfection.

And, of course, the setting was wonderful for illusions—the darkness outside, the beauty of the house, the open fireplace with a crackling fire.

She had removed her shoes and she wriggled her toes inside her socks. She did, she thought, somewhat let the side down with her faded jeans and oversized shirt. Pearls and cashmere would have been far more suitable to the setting, but that didn't bother her.

Nicholas was now descending the ladder and he and Amy stood back to look at the tree.

'Too many ornaments of the same colour on that branch,' he said at last. He looked over his shoulder to where Leigh was sitting on the ground, and waved his finger in an admonishing fashion. 'You could have told us!'

'I hate repeating myself,' Leigh said with a grin, 'and, anyway, I'm getting accustomed to the top-heavy look. I think it's a novel approach to decorating a tree.'

'What about the presents?' Amy asked hopefully.

'Santa hasn't come yet,' Leigh said. She looked at her watch. 'He's not due down that chimney for a few hours yet.'

'No, I don't mean *those* presents. I mean the ones from my friends in London.'

'OK, you can go fetch them,' Leigh told her lazily, 'but make it quick. It's bedtime soon.'

'Already?'

'I'm afraid so. Little girls need lots of sleep so that they're nice and rested in the morning!'

'But she *could* stay up a little later tonight,' Nicholas said. 'Couldn't she?'

Their combined charm was enough, Leigh thought, to produce an instant headache.

'Well, maybe an extra half-hour can be tacked on!'

So then came the presents, little parcels from Amy's friends at school and two from family friends. She placed them carefully at the bottom of the tree, dispersing them so that they looked more substantial.

Leigh thought that with very little effort she could fall asleep. In fact, her eyes were beginning to feel quite heavy when the door to the sitting room was pushed open and two people swept into the room, two people who stood in the middle of all the disarray, their eyes seeking out first Nicholas, then Amy.

'Nicholas!' The woman's voice was sharp and well bred, and although she was breathing quickly, as though she'd been in a rush, she was still immaculately coiffeured. She was wearing a long-sleeved woollen dress in navy blue, and a pair of navy blue flat shoes with a thin white strip of leather piping in the middle. She was tall and well built, but not overweight.

Leigh, who had shot to her feet the moment the couple had walked in, knew instantly who they were, and a flare of panic swept through her.

She didn't look at Nicholas. She looked at Amy, who caught her eye and nervously rushed to her.

'Mother! Dad... What in God's name are you two doing here?'

For perhaps the first time since she had met him he looked utterly disconcerted, but only for an instant, then he moved towards his parents and kissed his mother on the cheek.

'What are you doing here?' he asked, in a flatter, calmer voice.

'Nicholas!' His mother held him at arm's length and looked at him critically. His father, who had adopted a less dramatic approach, stood behind his wife and placed his hands on her shoulders. He was as tall as his son, and as striking to look at—the older counterpart, with greying hair and an austere face.

'I think we need to sit down,' he said. 'Come along, Hilary, the last thing we need now is a scene.'

Amy clutched Leigh's hands tightly in her own, well aware of the atmosphere but unable to decipher where it sprang from.

'We had a rather mysterious telephone call from

Fiona,' Nicholas's father was saying as they lowered themselves onto the sofa. They both looked at Amy when he said this.

'Leigh, I think it would be wise if you take Amy upstairs now.'

Leigh gripped her niece's hand and nodded. No introductions had been made and she knew why. They both knew who Amy was and they knew who she was as well. Heaven only knew what Fiona had told them, but she would have bet her life that none of it had been complimentary.

Well, she and Nicholas had been destined to a brief affair but, with his parents sitting there, looking at her, it appeared that stillborn would have been a better description.

'Please come back down when Amy's in bed,' he told her as she walked past him, and she nodded again.

'Are those Nicholas's mum and dad?' Amy asked as soon as they were out of the room. 'What are they doing here? You never said that they would be coming.'

'Perhaps they thought that they'd surprise us,' Leigh said distractedly.

'Nicholas didn't seem very pleased.'

'I'm sure he is.' She wondered what he would be telling them, how they would be handling this unexpected situation. Well, Fiona had been true to her word. She hadn't accepted her dismissal from Nicholas's life, lying down. She had decided that if she had to go then she would create merry hell in the process.

She must have also suspected that, faced with his parents' disapproval, he would almost certainly dump Leigh, whom he had no intentions of marrying anyway. He would not put up a fight for a woman who only interested him as a sexual partner.

She heard herself talking to her niece, answering her questions, but her mind was a thousand miles away. There was a dull feeling of resignation inside her.

Given the choice, she would have remained in the bedroom and left them to get on with it, but she couldn't. Apart from Nicholas's request for her to return, she knew that she had to go back to find out what lay in store for Amy.

His mother seemed somewhat calmer by the time Leigh returned. It was still an awkward situation, though. There was silence as she walked in and sat down, then Hilary Kendall said, with supreme politeness, 'I gather you are the child's aunt.'

'Her name is Leigh, Mother.'

'I must tell you that I am quite overwhelmed by all this.'

'Fiona,' Nicholas explained in a hard voice, 'apparently telephoned my parents as soon as she left the house.'

'So you know,' Leigh said, addressing his mother, attempting not to look cowed by the situation, 'that Amy is your grandchild.'

'It's all quite unorthodox, my dear,' Mrs Kendall said. 'This really was *not* what we had in mind for our son at all.'

'But naturally we're delighted,' Nicholas's father intervened in a warning voice. 'We had both rather given up on this wayward son of ours producing an heir.'

'But not like *this*.' Mrs Kendall persisted.

'Well, Mother, you have two choices. You either accept it with dignity or you don't. It's up to you.'

'I'm afraid, Hilary, he's absolutely right.'

'The child does bear a striking resemblance to you when you were a boy,' Mrs Kendall conceded. 'But I don't give a fig what you boys say, this has been a terrible shock. I know you explained, Nicholas. I know you said that you were going to tell us everything but I feel very hurt—'

'For which I am truly sorry, Mother, but there's no point dwelling on all of that. It's done.'

'And you, my dear,' Mrs Kendall said, shifting so that she could now incorporate Leigh within her line of vision. 'I gather you've been employed by my son to look after his daughter.'

'I do happen to be related to the child in question,' Leigh answered coolly.

'Fiona has told us quite a bit about you—'

'If you have any sense at all, Mother, you'll disregard every word. I've been through with you just now why Fiona did what she did.'

'But I would still like to know,' Mrs Kendall said, 'and so would your father, what exactly this woman is to you. You'll forgive me, my dear,' she carried on, inclining her body towards Leigh, 'but as Fiona was at great pains to point out, we don't know a thing about you.'

'I quite understand,' Leigh said in a composed voice. 'Well, to fill you in, my parents are both dead, I have no family to speak of, no money, aside from a derisory amount of savings, and no lineage. I have never skied in winter or done St Tropez in summer. This is the first grand house I have ever set foot inside. I have never lived in a house with more than three bedrooms.

'I was an impoverished art student before I got Amy and found myself a pitiful office job, and as from January I will return to being an art student. In other words, I'm terribly proud of my background and I have no complaints about my life.' She realised that she was leaning forward, perched on the edge of the chair, gripping both sides of it with her fingers.

Mrs Kendall smiled, and Leigh glimpsed some of the charm that her son had inherited. 'But, my dear, all that aside, how do you feel about gardens?'

'Oh, gardens?' Leigh smiled back. 'Yes, I love them.'

'Is that résumé quite enough for you, Mother?' Nicholas asked, 'because I hope to persuade this girl to be my wife.'

CHAPTER TEN

AFTER his parents had left the room Nicholas came and sat next to Leigh on the sofa.

Had he told his parents that he was going to marry her? Had he? Had she misheard or had the statement been some sort of upper-class joke?

He had told his parents, gently but firmly, that perhaps they ought to get some sleep, and that he needed to talk to Leigh. That had been only five minutes ago, if that, but it felt as though several hours had passed since his extraordinary announcement.

There was a gap of about two feet between them on the sofa. She felt like the prim star of a black and white movie, preserving an air of decorum in the midst of emotional tumult.

'Well?' he asked her, sprawling back against the chair and stretching out his arm along the back. 'Have you nothing at all to say?'

'I'm lost for words,' Leigh replied.

'I take it that's a no in response to my proposal?' He didn't look at her when he said this. He stared into the distance and idly drummed his fingers against the back of the sofa.

'Why?'

'Why?' He finally looked at her. '*Why?* You make it sound as though the thought of someone proposing to you is as unlikely as a trip to the moon.'

'That's not what I mean and you know it, Nicholas!' Leigh told him impatiently. 'If I recall a certain conversation you had with Fiona not so long ago, you said that you weren't looking for commitment. So I don't understand—'

'It makes sense, don't you think?'

'*What* makes sense?'

'Us.' He shrugged and looked away again briefly. 'I personally believe that a child needs a family unit, and you and I can provide Amy with a family. I'm her natural father and you're her aunt—what could be better?'

What, indeed.

'I've watched the two of you together. You have a…bond, a natural bond. It would be hard to find anyone who could provide that.'

'So, let me get this straight. Your proposal is more along the lines of a business proposition, is that it?' She could feel her temper rising. 'You've carefully weighed up the pros and cons and decided that I would be a suitable candidate for marriage, with Amy in mind.' She rose abruptly and began to pace the room, clenching and unclenching her fists as she walked.

'Why not? It's hardly as though we don't get along.'

'What you mean is it's hardly as though we haven't already slept together!'

She paused by the mantelpiece, stared at him and then resumed her restless pacing.

'Think about it logically! If we don't get married, you'll eventually leave to get on with your own life and you'll also eventually lose touch with Amy. Perhaps not immediately, but in time. The visits will become fewer and further between, you'll meet someone, settle down, have a family of your own and the bond you have now with Amy will be broken for ever. As for me, I'll get married. I might even leave the country to settle somewhere else.'

'You're going to live abroad? Since when have you been formulating this plan?'

'I haven't been formulating any plan! I'm merely putting forward possible scenarios.'

'So.' She walked across to where he was sitting and stood in front of him with her hands on her hips. 'We get married. Amy's as happy as a little bean in a bean bag, and what about us? Or, rather, what about me? I take it this little plan involves us sleeping together, and then, presumably, when you get bored with me you can feel free to look outside for other...distractions!'

'Would that bother you?'

Would that bother her? The thought of it was enough to make her feel ill. Here he sat, coolly planning a life of convenient cohabitation. Convenient, at any rate, for him. A nightmare from her point of view. She couldn't imagine anything worse than having to spend the rest of her days living with Nicholas and watching from the sidelines as he got on with his life. Preserving the veneer of the perfect marriage for the sake of his daughter.

'I'm going to have to refuse your offer,' she said tightly, 'logical though it sounds. There's more to marriage than logic.'

'You're a twentieth-century woman, Leigh. You told me so yourself! You're not looking for commitment. Why should you be so bothered by a marriage of convenience when the benefits are so apparent? Aside from anything else, you'll be able to enjoy all the privileges that money can buy—'

'I don't give a hang about your money! You know that!' The suggestion that she might somehow be talked into his scheme by the promise of being able to enjoy his wealth was an insult. 'You don't understand, do you?' she demanded, shaking. 'You've spent your life cooped up in your ivory tower, untroubled by ever having to invest your emotions in anything! You think that you can run every aspect of your life according to rules and reason and logic and practicality!'

'Why are you acting as though my proposal of marriage is a slap in your face?'

'Because it is! When I think about a marriage proposal I think—'

'About declarations of love? Adoration? Worship?'

'Yes, as a matter of fact, I do!' she snapped. 'Do you have a problem with that?'

'So if I had asked you to marry me because I loved you then you would have accepted.'

'That's beside the point.' She began to walk away, not caring for this turn in the conversation, but he reached out and snapped his fingers around her wrist so that she was forced to remain where she was.

'OK. I love you. Will you marry me?'

'There's no need to tell lies, Nicholas.'

He remained quiet for so long that in the end she looked down at him but she couldn't see the expression on his face, which was turned away.

It was funny how still it was in the room. She had only really just noticed it. They had drawn the curtains earlier on, and she imagined what it was like outside— cold and windy, with that lovely smell of Christmas. Amy was upstairs in bed, sound asleep, dreaming the sweet dreams of the innocent.

'No lies,' he muttered brusquely, and she bent a little to try and catch what he was saying.

'What?'

'I said, it seems that...' He stared up at her, then gently lowered her onto the sofa next to him. 'It seems that...' he began once more. 'I don't know how this happened... I never banked on anything like this...but it would appear that...'

'What are you trying to say?' She could hear the fierce beating of her heart, like a steady drum roll inside her.

'I'm trying to say...that, yes...I do...'

'Do...love me...?'

'Before you start refusing me, I realise that you're still young, I realise that there are things that you might want to do with your life—your art, a career perhaps. I know that. I am not one of these men who would stand in your way. And before you tell me that you don't want commitment, that you don't love me, just hear me out. You could learn to love me. I feel it.' He had said all this in a tremendous rush, barely meeting her eyes but still with his fingers fastened tightly around her wrist.

'Learn? Learn to love you?'

'Is that beyond the bounds of possibility?' He shot her a dark, challenging look and she lowered her eyes.

'How can you *learn* to love someone?' she asked. She felt giddy, blissfully giddy. Was she dreaming? If she was then she hoped that she never woke up. She touched the side of his face gently with one finger.

'Falling in love is like suddenly being run over by a steamroller. No time to get used to the idea. It just sort of sweeps around you in a rush so that all of a sudden nothing matters any more. I should know. It's how I've felt about you for a long time. For ever.'

He smiled that smile of his. That slow, wonderful smile of his. The one that could make her heart do somersaults.

'Why didn't you say?' he murmured, caressing her nape with his fingers. 'Why didn't you tell me? I thought I told you that you were supposed to tell me everything?' He leaned forward and kissed her, a soft, melting kiss that was in no hurry to end. With a sigh, Leigh wrapped her arms around his neck.

'If I'm sleeping,' she said softly, 'then please don't pinch me. Please let me sleep on.'

'I love you, Leigh. I don't know when it happened, but you stopped being a complete stranger who had somehow managed to turn my world upside down and became someone who was indispensable. At first I told myself that I found you indispensable because you were Amy's aunt, because you were a bridge to my daughter. But the fact was that you got under my skin.

'I started thinking about you night and day. I couldn't wait to rush back from work so that I could see your face and hear your voice. I suddenly discovered that short hair and a stubborn face and jeans and baggy jumpers were the most beautiful things in the world.'

He kissed her neck and she felt a pulsing throb of desire course through her. She would never doubt the existence of miracles again.

'Are you sure?' she asked anxiously. 'What about Fiona, the things she said? We *are* from different worlds, you know.'

'Thank goodness for that. I would hate to marry a clone of myself. And, besides, I've long given up the party life. I don't mix with the champagne-drinking crowd, despite the standard of my lifestyle. These things can be deceptive, you know. The fact is I've buried myself in my work.

'When you showed up at my club with the prospect of a daughter I never knew I'd fathered I was horrified, but I was curious as well. It was only when you and Amy became such a big part of my life that I finally realised what I had been missing.'

'Your parents... What will they think?'

'They'll think that it's high time some unfortunate woman came along to get their son off their hands. Normally the marriage comes before the child, but they'll accept it all better than you think. Besides, my mother likes you and that's half the battle won.'

Leigh laughed throatily. 'She certainly has a unique way of disguising the fact.'

'You warranted a smile from her. Quite something, I assure you. I gather she used to be quite the feisty sort when she married my father. She appreciates the quality.' His hands travelled under her jumper to cup her breasts and she shuddered with pleasure. 'Of course, not half as much as I do.'

'I'm not as good-looking as Fiona,' Leigh told him. 'I'm not as elegant or sophisticated.'

'You underestimate yourself, my darling.'

It was the first term of endearment she had ever heard him utter, and it felt so natural to hear it that she gave a shiver of pleasure.

His fingers played with her nipples and she felt them stiffen at his touch. He raised her jumper, and she leaned back so that his mouth could gently caress her breasts. A slow, delicate teasing.

'Not here,' she murmured, tugging his head up and kissing his lips. 'Not with your parents in the house!'

He pulled away from her and laughed. 'Why? Do you think they're outside the door, listening for any sounds of foul play?'

'They might well be!' She giggled at the thought of it.

'I guess I can hold out,' he said, 'at least for the moment. Just.'

'And we really ought to get to bed. Give that chubby chap with the white beard an opportunity to do his stuff.'

'Or else he might just forget. He might just get a little too carried away with the mistress of the house.'

It was idyllic. The lights on the Christmas tree were winking in the semi-darkened room, and the presents were brought out and laid beneath it.

There was no need for Amy to wake her up the following morning. Leigh was up and about before six with curtains pulled back, watching the hesitant flurries of snow outside.

'It's snowing!'

Leigh looked around and smiled at her niece. 'Just another little something Santa thought he'd bring for you.'

'I wonder what else he's brought us,' Amy said, tugging her hand.

'Possibly more than you think.'

There was a knock on the door, and they both watched as Nicholas entered the room.

'Merry Christmas, little one,' he said, lifting Amy into the air and depositing a kiss on her cheek. He set her back on her feet and turned to Leigh. 'Merry Christmas, big one,' he said, smiling. He touched her face and then kissed her lightly on the mouth. Then he looked at her and she nodded, reading his intentions and knowing the moment had come.

So they sat Amy down and told her. Very gently, very carefully.

'You're my dad?' she said at the end of it all, and Nicholas nodded. 'Do I call you Dad?'

'Nicholas is fine by me. What feels right to you is right for me.'

Leigh smiled as she watched various expressions flit over her niece's face—astonishment, frowning consideration, a dawning delight.

'I had a daddy when I was younger,' she said eventually. 'Now I think I'll have a dad.'

'And a Leigh,' Leigh said, hugging her.

'And a mum,' Amy said, smiling. 'It makes it easier.'

'And grandparents who are dying to see you to get to know you,' Leigh said, looking at Nicholas over the top of Amy's head.

Amy smiled, as the concept of all this family settled in. 'Now,' she said pragmatically, 'can we go down? I want to see what Santa brought me!'

Take 2 bestselling love stories FREE

Plus get a FREE surprise gift!

Special Limited-Time Offer

Mail to Harlequin Reader Service®

3010 Walden Avenue
P.O. Box 1867
Buffalo, N.Y. 14240-1867

YES! Please send me 2 free Harlequin Presents® novels and my free surprise gift. Then send me 6 brand-new novels every month, which I will receive months before they appear in bookstores. Bill me at the low price of $3.12 each plus 25¢ delivery and applicable sales tax, if any*. That's the complete price, and a saving of over 10% off the cover prices—quite a bargain! I understand that accepting the books and gift places me under no obligation ever to buy any books. I can always return a shipment and cancel at any time. Even if I never buy another book from Harlequin, the 2 free books and the surprise gift are mine to keep forever.

106 HEN CH69

Name	(PLEASE PRINT)
Address	Apt. No.
City	State	Zip

This offer is limited to one order per household and not valid to present Harlequin Presents® subscribers. *Terms and prices are subject to change without notice. Sales tax applicable in N.Y.

UPRES-98

Toast the special events in your life with Harlequin Presents®!

With the purchase of *two* Harlequin Presents®
BIG EVENT books, you can send in for two sparkling
plum-colored Wineglasses. A retail value of $19.95!

ACT NOW TO COLLECT
TWO BEAUTIFUL WINEGLASSES!

On the official proof-of-purchase coupon below, fill in your name,
address and zip or postal code and send it, plus $2.99 U.S./$3.99 CAN.
for postage and handling (check or money order—please do not send
cash) payable to Harlequin Books, to: In the U.S.: 3010 Walden
Avenue, P.O. Box 9077, Buffalo, N.Y. 14269-9077; In Canada: P.O. Box
609, Fort Erie, Ontario L2A 5X3. Please allow 4-6 weeks for delivery.
Order your set of wineglasses now! Quantities are limited. Offer for
the Plum Wineglasses expires December 31, 1998.

HARLEQUIN®
Makes any time special ™

Coming Next Month

HARLEQUIN PRESENTS®

THE BEST HAS JUST GOTTEN BETTER!

#1995 MARRIED BY CHRISTMAS Carole Mortimer
Lilli was mortified when she woke up in Patrick Devlin's bed!
He wasn't about to let her forget it, either. Patrick would
save her father's chain of hotels...if she married him—by
Christmas!

#1996 THE BRIDAL BED Helen Bianchin
(Do Not Disturb)
For her mother's wedding, Suzanne and her ex-fiancé, Sloan,
had to play the part of a happy, soon-to-marry couple! After
sharing a room—and a bed!—their pretend passion became
real...and another wedding was on the agenda!

#1997 BABY INCLUDED! Mary Lyons
(The Big Event!)
Lord Ratcliffe was delighted that Eloise had turned up at
his surprise birthday party. He'd always thought she
was an ordinary American tourist; but in fact she was an
international sex symbol...and secretly carrying his baby!

#1998 A HUSBAND'S PRICE Diana Hamilton
Six years ago when Adam and Claudia had split up, he'd left
a part of himself with her—a child. Now Adam's help comes
with a hefty price tag—that Claudia become his wife. Faced
with bankruptcy and a custody battle, Claudia has no
choice....

#1999 A NANNY FOR CHRISTMAS Sara Craven
(Nanny Wanted!)
Dominic Ashton thought Phoebe was a wonderful stand-in
mom for little Tara; it was a pity she couldn't stay longer.
But Phoebe had her reasons for going: if Dominic had
forgotten their first meeting years before, she certainly
hadn't!

#2000 MORGAN'S CHILD Anne Mather
(Harlequin Presents' 2000th title!)
Four years after the death of her husband in war-torn Africa,
Felicity Riker at last had a new man...a new life. Then she
heard that Morgan had been found *alive*...and that he was
on his was back to reclaim his long-lost wife....